+10⁵

THE WINTER ROAD

The Winter Road

Terry Hokenson

FRONT STREET
Asheville, North Carolina

ACKNOWLEDGMENTS

Those who generously gave valuable advice, information, and feedback in the shaping of this story are too many to be named. I wish to give special thanks, however, to Jane Resh Thomas, my esteemed mentor, teacher, and friend, who nudged this book from pipe dream to possibility.

Library of Congress Cataloging-in-Publication Data

Hokenson, Terry, 1948–
The winter road / Terry Hokenson.— 1st ed.
p. cm.
Summary: Seventeen-year-old Willa, still grieving over the death of her older brother and the neglect of her father, decides to fly a small plane to fetch her mother in Northern Ontario, but when the plane crashes she is all alone in the snowy wilderness.
ISBN 1-932425-45-4 (alk. paper)
[1. Survival—Fiction. 2. Canada—Fiction.] I. Title.
PZ7.H6873Win 2006
[Fic]—dc22   2005027030

Front Street
An Imprint of Boyds Mills Press, Inc.
A Highlights Company

815 Church Street
Honesdale, Pennsylvania 18431

to Alberta

1

The Hammer

Willa Raedl walked into her fifth-period shop class at Sioux Lookout High School, took her knight's helmet from the rack, and placed it on the steel bench where she'd been welding it together for the past two weeks. She hated it. It looked like a bucket that had tangled with a lawnmower. She fingered the collar plate, walked to the tool crib, and returned with a large sledgehammer.

"That's a bit stout to straighten it with, isn't it, eh?" said Mark, her bench mate.

She nodded, calmly swung the sledge in a high arc over her head, and slammed it down on the helmet. The blow resounded on the metal bench like a cannon shot, and the mangled mass bounced with a tinny crash on the floor. Startled shouts, laughter, and chatter boiled up as Willa set the hammer down and strode out.

"What's the problem, Willa?" called Mr. Beamish as he followed her into the hall.

"It was a piece of crap!" she yelled, disappearing into the girls' restroom.

She locked herself in a stall, curled her fingers over the top of the door, and pushed her forehead into the cold metal.

"But Willa," Mr. Beamish called through the door, "you were doing fine!"

"It was garbage!" cried Willa. Under her breath she added, "It was bloody stupid and pointless." She sat down on the toilet, head in her hands.

"What's that, Sport? Willa, come on out," pleaded Mr. Beamish. "Maybe there's something else going on, eh? Let's talk."

Beamer was a nice man, but she couldn't take any more well-meant advice. She'd had weekly counseling sessions with Miss Gant for a year after her brother Ray died. Over the next five years she was in and out of counselors' offices. A couple of years ago Jean had even driven her to Dryden twice a month to see Dr. Downey, an honest-to-God shrink.

"Willa?"

"I'll be *fine*, Mr. Beamish."

She had to get away, go climb a mountain or something. She thought of driving west to Winnipeg, but she didn't know anyone there and a city that size was intimidating—last year she'd gone on a class trip to the Manitoba Museum of Man and Nature. Besides, her car was a twelve-year-old Blazer. It wasn't up to a six-hour road trip, especially in January. It might get her there and then not get her back. Maybe she could take a train—Sioux Lookout lay on the Canadian National Railway.

Willa quietly left the stall and listened at the door, then cracked it open. Mr. Beamish was gone—probably calling the office for help. She bolted out and collided with her friend Jackie Leveque.

"Willa, are you okay?" Jackie asked, her voice tight.

"Jackie," Willa said, gripping the taller girl's arms and looking directly into her eyes, "I'm fine, I just need to get out of here. But thanks."

"Take care, eh?" said Jackie.

Willa walked quickly to her locker, grabbed her coat and daypack, and left the building.

At home she packed her duffel bag. She'd ride along with her uncle Jordy after all, she decided. He was taking the Cessna 185 to Peawanuck, a Cree village near Hudson Bay, to pick up her mom. They could just pop one of the back seats in again so all three could fit when they picked Jean up.

Jordy was planning to leave at the ungodly hour of 5:30 a.m., so Willa had taken a pass. Besides, he was going on a Thursday and she would have to miss school—she was already on probation for too many absences.

She was fed up with school. Forced to learn things she didn't care about, and not allowed to study things she did. She never seemed to get in step with the program.

Only two or three of her classes had any juice in them. Chemistry rocked. Ellie Campbell made everything connect, and Willa loved the labs. Her literature teacher, Arthur Wegamow, otherwise known as Woogy, played keyboard in a jazz band. He would slip her a good read now and then. The latest had been a novel by native author Ruby Slipperjack, who lived in Thunder Bay.

History, math, all the rest—except her industrial arts shop

class—left her cold. She was in no danger of graduating with honors.

Periodically the big wave swept over her and she couldn't even breathe. Friends would tease her, "Earth to Willa," because she was in another world. She didn't have much to say at those times. She dreamed of traveling, discovering new places and new people. Surely something out there had more music in it than her life in tiny Sioux Lookout.

Willa got up off her bed, kicked the duffel bag down the stairs, and put a block of frozen venison stew in a pot on the stove to heat.

The night before, while she was warming another of Jean's homemade frozen dinners, Bud's pickup had pulled into the driveway. He was home again after ten days away. The back door opened and Bud's leather bag thudded on the floor of the mudroom, followed by a slam and stomping. "Anybody home?" he called.

Willa was ladling herself a bowl of the chicken and wild rice soup when he appeared in the doorway. "Want some?" she asked.

"Not right now," he answered. "What's up?"

"Not much," Willa murmured, sitting down to eat, not looking at him.

He paused a moment. "Where's Jean?" he asked.

"Peawanuck," she said, stirring her soup. "You didn't know that?"

Bud paused again. "Something wrong?"

"Like what?" Willa said, lowering her spoon.

"You don't have much to say."

"Why should I?" she said hotly. "You're the one who's gone all the time. You should be *full* of news."

She rose and walked quickly upstairs. At the top landing she said under her breath, "Gimme a break. You don't care what I have to say."

She had locked herself in her room then, sat on the bed, and gripped the edge of the mattress in both hands. Her clock radio was playing two stations at low volume. She didn't really expect much from Bud anymore. He never came to see her hockey matches or theater performances. Having to work on her Blazer would put him in a foul mood. She'd learned to do all the routine stuff herself—changing the oil, replacing the fan belt—just so she wouldn't have to ask Bud for help. Besides, Ray would have worked on his own car himself.

An hour later the back door had slammed and Bud was off again.

Willa finished eating and called Karin.

"How's it going with both of your parents gone?" Karin asked.

Willa belched. "It's okay. Bud came home last night and left after about an hour."

"Where'd he go this time?" asked Karin.

"He took some people on a big dogsled adventure. Whatever." She hadn't been on a trip in the bush with Bud since Ray died.

"You okay?" Karin asked. "Tony told me you woke up everybody in shop today."

"Eh, I was tired of my project."

"You're not worried about your grade? I mean, now you'll just get an F, right?"

"You know I don't give a pot of warm piss about grades, Karin."

"But you didn't have to smash it."

"But Karin, it felt so bloody *good!*" They both laughed.

"I gotta go, Willa—rehearsal tonight."

"Okay. Break a leg."

At 4:30 a.m. Willa dressed, slipped quietly out the back door with her duffel bag, and got in the Blazer.

If I had a penis and a set of balls, Dad, then would you give a rat's ass about me?

The Blazer knew the eight miles to Jordy's place on Copper Lake by heart. Willa pulled in beside the station wagon and walked down the slope to the back. Jordy sometimes parked the Cessna there on the ice in winter. Since it wasn't there now, it would be at the airport three miles east, where Jordy shared a hangar with other pilots.

Lights were on inside; Willa knocked and walked in, calling his name. She found him sacked out on the sofa. "Jordy? Jordy?"

She couldn't rouse him. A half-empty bottle of Crown Royal stood on the table amid dirty dishes and newspapers.

"Holy Godzilla," she murmured. "Jordy, what have you done?" His eyelids made her think of naked baby birds. From his open mouth came soft snores and whisky fumes. Obviously he couldn't fly. Even when she kicked the leg of the couch, Jordy didn't stir.

"Don't you disappear on me like Bud, Jordy," she said. This wasn't like him—something must have happened.

She crossed her arms, fists in her armpits, tears brimming. Left to her own devices again. How would Jean get to Kasabonika? She could lose her grant. She'd worked two years to get it.

Willa could do it. Jordy couldn't fly, but she could. Should she call somebody? For God's sake, it wasn't even five a.m. yet. She couldn't call anybody at that hour. Besides, it wasn't such a big deal—Jordy trusted her to fly solo.

She left a note. *Jordy—I couldn't wake you up. I am taking the 185 to Peawanuck so Jean won't be stuck. I'll just go on your flight plan. Don't worry. See you when I get back. Love, Willa.*

She jumped into the Blazer and headed for the airport.

2

Flying to Peawanuck

Willa buckled herself into the cockpit of the little ski plane as its engine warmed to a high keen in the early morning darkness. Checklist completed, she tuned in the mechanical voice of the northern Ontario flight service broadcast. It repeated: *Sioux Lookout information echo, 1145 Zulu, wind five zero at ten to twelve steady, sky condition clear . . .*

Willa set the altimeter. Flaps were down for takeoff.

She bit her lip. Uncle Jordy would slam his watch cap on the floor and stomp on it when he found out. But he had gotten drunk at the wrong time, and he'd know it. Jean would steam and twist her hair in her fingers, but she'd realize that Willa was saving her program. No question, it was the right thing to do. And she could do it. She'd show them. Maybe Bud would sit up and pay attention, tell her how proud he was of his daughter.

Cabin heat was flowing now, and Willa pushed her parka hood back. Her thick dark brown hair bushed out, full of static in the dry air. She gathered it together, gave it a twist, and pushed it down the back of her collar.

Easing the throttle forward, she taxied the roaring aircraft toward the runway. High banks of plowed snow shone like craggy mountain peaks under the floodlamps. Her landing lights probed the broken white edges of the airfield and the dark fringe of spruce forest beyond.

She hadn't exactly talked Jordy into this, and he wasn't exactly in any shape to say no. But why would he? He'd trained her himself. Sure, she was just seventeen, but she had been a licensed pilot for three years now. And she'd flown solo to Cat Lake and Fort Hope just last summer.

Willa called to activate the flight plan. She positioned the plane for takeoff, pulled the throttle back, and paused, scanning the night sky. All clear.

She pushed the throttle up all the way. The whine of the engine took on a commanding thrum that reached through the yoke in her hands to the seat of her pants. The Cessna pulled smoothly forward and quickly developed a rumbling sprint as the blue lights raced by. The rumbling broke off as the white hopper lifted into the night. The engine noise in the cabin softened. Her anger morphed into the thrill of flying. Piloting an airplane was hellacool. She had a mission.

Willa climbed steadily. Banking the plane in the direction of Pickle Lake, a frontier town 150 miles north-northeast, she raised the flaps and watched the altimeter needle reach 2,000 feet, then 3,000. The lights of the sleeping town of Sioux Lookout glimmered behind her as she burrowed into the starlit darkness.

Alarm returned to Willa's throat. Jordy! She'd never known him to get so trashed as to miss a scheduled run. Jordy was by the clock and by the book; everyone said so. What had happened? He'd been her buddy, started taking her on freight runs the summer after Ray died.

Ah, Ray. She focused on her instruments.

She had more than four hundred miles to fly over a wilderness of black spruce, lakes, and marshes to Peawanuck, which was on the Winisk River just thirty miles inland from Hudson Bay. Three and a half or four hours, depending on the winds. She'd arrive around 9:30 a.m., in plenty of time to get Jean to Kasabonika before dark. Now Willa understood why Jordy planned to leave so early.

Ray—he'd be twenty-one now, maybe off somewhere, but he'd be there when she needed him. She flashed back to the moment when Bud crashed into the kitchen from the mudroom, his face all red and twisted, and punched the refrigerator. Little magnets flew.

"Ray's dead. Hit a tree on the Ski-Doo."

Jean had dropped to the floor. Willa had been eleven then, six years ago.

She checked her watch—6:05 a.m. The eastern sky would begin to lighten in an hour. Sunrise at 7:52. Full daylight lasted barely eight hours in mid-January.

Willa leveled the Cessna at a cruising altitude of 5,000 feet, airspeed 130 knots. She gave the light northwest headwind its due and crabbed the plane toward it to maintain her heading to Pickle Lake, roughly 125 miles north-northeast.

Bud had quit drinking when Ray died. But he'd disappeared too. Spent more and more time in the bush. Sure, he made his living as a wilderness guide, but he went off on his own a lot too. Just wasn't there.

School was hell that spring. Most of the time she floated

through her classes like a sleepwalker, but sometimes she rico-
cheted between hysterical laughter and volcanic anger. When
summer vacation came, Willa felt some relief, but the birds
weren't singing quite on key. There was no Ray to follow around,
and no Bud either.

"Your uncle Jordy wants to talk to you, Willa," said Jean one
day in June, after spending a few quiet minutes on the phone.

"Hello, sweetheart," Jordy had said. "Say, I have a bit of a
long flight up to Big Trout tomorrow, and since school's over for
the summer, I thought maybe you wouldn't mind keeping me
company, eh?"

That was how it started.

The plane droned on in the night. The moonless sky was velvet
black, and the stars were intense. The left wing above obscured
her view of the Big Dipper, but ahead lay the constellation
Cassiopeia, the Woman in the Chair. Willa looked out the side
window. A mile below, the snow-mantled Ontario wilderness
was a ghostly platter that melted into the inky sky all around.

Jordy had stepped in for Bud. He'd taught her about navigation, showed her the constellations, tried to explain things—well,
things that were beyond his powers of explanation, like why her
father acted the way he did. The way he ignored her.

Buckling herself into the co-pilot's seat beside her uncle had
been new. Before that she'd ridden in the back a few times. "The
steering wheel is called a 'yoke' in an airplane," Jordy explained.
"That one in front of you works just like mine." She watched it
mimic the yoke in Jordy's hands. Before long he had her trying

it and feeling the response of the plane as it rolled left or right, climbed or descended.

Over the summer they flew together often. All along Jordy slipped little bits of lore and information to Willa, so she hardly noticed when he began giving her serious flight lessons.

"She talked me into it," he told Jean with a grin, winking at Willa.

Jean shook her head. "Willa, honey, be careful." She treated Willa like glass.

"Ray woulda liked this part, wouldn't he," Jordy had said on the day Willa made her first landing. The comment rang like a bell. From then on, she couldn't get enough of flying. Ray's bravado became her courage. Flying a plane was frightening, all right. But Willa had become fascinated with flying over the rim of death. She found calm in the mechanics of the plane and navigated through her fear with her hands on the yoke.

Now Willa reached back for her duffel bag and hauled it over into the co-pilot's seat. She fished a hair tie out of the bag and made a ponytail to keep her hair out of her face. The Cessna was a four-seater, but the two back seats had been removed to make more room for cargo. Boxes of supplies bound for the nursing station took up half the cargo space.

Jean's workshop contract meant spending a week in each of four villages—Peawanuck, Kasabonika, Weagamow Lake, and Summer Beaver—with a week at home between Kasabonika and Weagamow Lake. Jordy was supposed to shuttle her from one to the next. But he had drunk himself out of this trip.

Heaving a sigh, Willa reached down and switched to the right wing tank to help balance the weight of the fuel. She glanced at her watch. A little over halfway to Pickle. She checked the altimeter and made a slight correction to her heading. A little shift in the wind. Right tank fuel needle was hardly off the full mark yet, but she would need to top up in Pickle Lake, because the trip to Peawanuck would push the limits of the Cessna's range.

Willa yawned and then sneezed. Her throat was a little scratchy. Ripples in the airstream gently drummed the wings. Probably some early shock waves of the cold front. She looked at the amp gauge. It read a little high. Hmm. She couldn't think of a reason that would be a problem. She maintained her course. Jean needed her supplies and had to get to Kasabonika. Besides, Willa was carrying stuff for the nursing station too, important cargo. A chill ran up her back as she thought about what she was doing.

She would show them. She had the skill and the nerve to do what needed to be done. Bud would see.

Ray. He'd had no fear. Bud had been proud of him.

Willa approached the tiny outpost of Pickle Lake on the frontier of the wilderness. Pickle lay as far north as paved roads went in Ontario. To the east she could make out a few ground lights. The New Osnaburgh Reserve, she guessed. She rolled the plane slightly to the left for a better view. The snow-covered lakes were just becoming distinct from the darker background of forest. Scattered flakes streaked by, illuminated by faint light from the east.

Willa radioed the Pickle Lake airport operator, who cleared her for an immediate landing. She brought the plane down and taxied to the fueling area.

A young man came out to help with the hose. Willa could tell he had questions, the way he kept looking at her.

"I'm Willa Raedl," she told him. "Jordy got sick, so I'm making a run to Peawanuck for him." She was so matter-of-fact about it that he just nodded and smiled. He knew Jordy well, she figured.

Back in the air, Willa tuned in local terminal information. The broadcast was broken and full of static—odd, when she was practically on top of the relay tower. *Four zero Zulu . . . visibility . . . cloud . . . one niner . . .* She listened through the repeated broadcast again. Apparently the front was expected to bring a cloud ceiling of 1,900 feet. Visibility was decreasing. Winter weather.

Pickle Lake was in almost a straight line from Sioux Lookout to Peawanuck. Willa had to turn only an additional degree or two to the east. The ride was getting bumpier. The front could mean tricky weather, even though the forecast sounded tame. She'd fly either under the ceiling or on top of the cloud deck, cross the front at right angles, and avoid most of the turbulence.

The accordion music at the wedding party last Saturday night went through her head. Jordy had gotten *so* drunk. She frowned. He and his friend from Red Lake had left together, leaning on each other. "They were pretty oiled," she said aloud, remembering.

Peawanuck. Female polar bears denned up around there in winter, gave birth during light hibernation, and moved with their cubs to the shore of Hudson Bay in spring. The males were out hunting on the sea ice in January. She wouldn't be seeing any on this trip.

Forty-five minutes beyond Pickle Lake, Willa met the front and dropped down to 1,800 feet to stay under the cloud ceiling.

Might as well see while there was anything to see, she figured. But the scattered flakes were turning gradually into a robust snowfall, hiding the horizon behind a curtain of powder. She was navigating again by instruments. She took a brief roll to the left to look straight down.

The ground was a disk of dim, mottled patches with edges that barely showed through the fog of falling snow, like a round gray tabletop that had been wiped with a wet cloth. The cloud layer above betrayed no relief or depth except in the foreground, where it formed a wispy bottom. Farther out in front of the plane, the cloud deck seamlessly merged in the haze with the gray disk below.

Keeping an eye on the instrument panel, Willa reached into her bag in the co-pilot's seat. She pulled out her thermos and mug and poured some hot tea.

She sneezed again, several times. There was a sharp odor in the cabin. It gnawed at her eyes and throat. Were exhaust fumes leaking into the heater shroud? Bloody old crate.

Willa reached over and shut off cabin heat. Better cold than poisoned. She slipped her hair tie off, pulled up her hood, and zipped her parka. She cracked open the vent overhead to let a little fresh air whistle in. Soon her breath was visible and steam rose from the mug.

The ceiling gradually dropped to 1,200 feet. Willa was uncomfortable cruising so low with the chance of wind shear, so she pulled back the yoke to climb above the clouds. She felt the pressure on her back as the nose came up. Rising into the cloud, she trimmed her tabs. The plane climbed, rocking, lofting, sinking in the undulating air.

After several minutes Willa came out on top at 6,500 feet. Two heartbeats later she plunged into a towering storm cloud. Suddenly she was in the bowels of darkness, in the green and purple coils of a raging serpent. The light aircraft swept to the right, then down, down, left, up, up, down. The mug popped out from between her knees. Willa wrestled for control, her eyes glued to the attitude indicator.

Thousands of hail pellets raked the aluminum skin of the plane with a roar. The Cessna vibrated as if it would come apart. The attitude indicator danced like the eyeball of a panicked horse. Instead of a pupil, its orb was imprinted with an airplane silhouette floating behind a thin horizon line. It rose and fell, rotated left and right, mirroring the motion of the plane. Willa had all she could do to respond to its cues. She plied the yoke left and right; the airplane veered one way and then another. Willa struggled now to bring the left wing up, now to get the nose down, now to avoid a stall, and so to dance with the storm. Her lips were pursed tight as a walnut.

She prayed for calm air. For long minutes the plane barreled along in the grip of the wind, with no regard to her intended heading. When the roiling chaos gave way at last to straight-line shock waves, Willa shot a look at her altimeter, then at her engine dials.

The instruments! Everything electrical was zeroed out.

Willa banged the panel with her gloved fist. Her lips went dry and her scalp prickled.

"Hey! Wake up in there!" she ordered, smacking the panel again. She got only the faintest crackling from the radio when she spun the tuning dial. Vital engine gauges were gone. She picked up the mike. The radio was dead. Fumes seared her eyes and throat.

Still, the engine sounded okay. Where was the nearest airstrip? And where was *she*? Without the radio she couldn't establish her location or bearing; she couldn't go anywhere. Tears brimmed in her burning eyes. She sucked in her breath. Yes—she'd have to put the crate down. Going on would just get her more lost.

The plane dodged on like a canoe caught in rapids. Willa hoped the ceiling below had not dropped any farther, for all she could do was scale down through the dense cloud and hope she had room to recover before she hit the trees. The airplane jigged, bucked, and creaked in the twisting wind.

The fumes grew unbearable. She opened the vent all the way, and icy air streamed in with a throaty moan. After an eternity, she dropped below the cloud deck and stabilized the plane.

The gale was stiff and snow-filled, but at least it was steady. She had less than eight hundred feet of altitude. Circling, she caught sight of a lake below that looked big enough. She checked her heading and started around for an approach into the wind.

The dense snowfall masked Willa's forward view. She could see only the dark trees beneath her. She wouldn't be able to see the end of her run till she was on the ground. Coming around on the leeward side of the lake, she descended within thirty feet of the treetops. She pushed her door open as far as she could—a couple of inches in the windstream—to ventilate the choking fumes. She looked down at trees rushing under and waited for the white edge of the lake to appear. When she saw it, she cut the fuel supply. A fire was the last thing she needed.

With her engine stilled, there was only the soughing of the aluminum airframe in the snowy wind. Willa brought the nose up and dropped the wing flaps.

The plane descended below the treetops, touched its skis down on the snow-covered lake, and bumped rapidly over the rolling drifts. Suddenly the shoreline rose out of the whiteness—too close! As trees rushed toward her, Willa steered for a dark hole, pulled her knees up, and covered her head with her arms.

With a violent shudder, metal snapped as a rocky ledge sheared off the landing gear. The plane plunged ahead on its belly through rasping brush into a crowd of black spruce. A thunderous jolt threw her against the seatbelt. Spraying snow, scraping branches, a hard jerk . . .

3

Down

Stunned, Willa slowly uncoiled herself. She raised her eyes to the shadows of black spruce boughs pressed against the windshield and realized that she was alive. Her heart was hammering. The blows spread through her head and her chest. Her tea came up and she lunged into the footwell. Spitting and gasping, she braced: *fire?* She must jump clear of the plane. She jerked her seatbelt release. Her door was jammed shut—tree limb—and the wing was gone! She went for the right door. That wing was gone too! So the fuel tanks were gone . . . Heavy waves of darkness enveloped her.

Vision returned. She grabbed the yoke and hung on to it, her breathing halting, gasping. After a few minutes the air came rhythmically. She felt a dull stinging over her left breast and groped inside her parka. Her sunglasses inside the pocket of her flight suit had been crushed by the seatbelt strap. She tossed the bent frame and lenses aside.

Turning around, she looked out the windows toward the rear of the plane. No fire. Willa closed her eyes and sank back into her seat. She flexed arms, legs, her body—nothing major felt wrong.

Awareness came and went in waves. She closed her eyes against another swell of dizziness. It passed. She studied her surroundings. Forward and left, the undersides of spruce branches. Out the rear to the right, the frozen lake dim in the blowing snow, brush along the near shore, aspen saplings and spruce trees. Dizzy.

Willa closed her eyes. Such a roar in her ears. A small taste of blood. Must have bitten her tongue. The wind groaned and snow seared the plane.

When she opened her eyes again, she looked more attentively around the tiny cabin. It was intact, although the windshield was badly cracked and the engine cowling crumpled. She'd come within inches of oblivion. The shearing of the skis, then the wings, slowed her down. The deep, snowplowing slide. Nose piled up against a tree. Supplies a jumble in the hold. A few small boxes had tumbled into the footwell of the co-pilot's seat.

Willa grabbed the microphone. Dead. The radio was gone, the power was gone.

She pulled the back of the co-pilot's seat forward and climbed into the cramped cargo area, moved boxes out of the way, and looked for the emergency locator transmitter.

I've crashed, I'm down! she screamed silently. The white spray, the thunderbolts, still hammered.

She forgot for a moment what she was looking for, then spotted a small vinyl box mounted on the wall and unlatched the cover.

It was empty. There was no emergency transmitter!

Willa stared at the empty box, then fumbled back to the left seat and sat down again. *No radio! No emergency transmitter!*

No way to call out.

The transmitter battery had to be replaced on a schedule. Had Jordy taken it out to replace the battery and forgotten to put it back? Maybe he was going to put it back when he left . . .

It was her fault! She should have checked!

She sat for a few minutes with her mind blank, massaging her scalp with her fingers, groping the chaos.

She drifted in and out of dreams. An hour passed. She opened her eyes.

Okay, this was just mechanical stuff. Okay. The radio didn't work—why? Because the power failed. What had cut the power—had a cable come loose? Short circuit? If she could find the problem, maybe she could fix it. She'd open the engine compartment.

She unlatched the right door and forced it open against the snow. She stepped out and sank to her thighs. She leaned back far enough to shut the door. The engine cowling was just a little too far away to reach from where she was, so she worked her legs to create a pit around herself and then gnawed at the snow with her feet until she stood beside the nose of the plane. The engine ticked as its metal parts bled their heat into the cold.

She lifted a spruce bough and raised the bent engine hood. A misshapen, smoking hulk greeted her where the battery was supposed to be. She squinted, coughed, and turned away. So that was where the fumes were coming from. What on earth would make a battery melt down like that?

The amp gauge! Did the meltdown have something to do with the high readings? Guilt hit her like a hammer. She had seen the danger and talked herself into ignoring it. It was all her fault!

However it had happened, Willa had no way to run the radio now.

Snow pellets stung her face. She climbed back into the plane and slammed the door shut. She caught her breath, fell quiet, looked out across the landscape into the maw of winter. Her fault. She had done it to herself. She felt heavy curtains fall over her.

She clasped her hands and pressed them against her forehead, pressed herself still.

Oh, God! She sat trembling.

The Cessna—a total loss. She had never come this close to being killed before. She saw the Ski-Doo smash into a tree again in her mind, and Ray lying dead in the snow. Suddenly the dam burst and Willa cried.

Everyone would think she was dead. *Stupid, stupid!* She cried so hard she thought her eyes would burst. Her whole body convulsed with the hot agony of her predicament, and she stiffened her legs against the floor of the footwell, pushing herself back into the seat as she pressed her bandana to her face.

Oh, God, was she going to die? *I'm sorry, I'm sorry,* she sobbed.

She went inert and wept softly. In the next ten minutes the bandana froze into a jagged red piece of cardboard, pliable only where it touched her face. As she sat motionless in her flight suit and parka, the first clue that she would not die right away sank in: she was getting cold.

The instinctive remedy for that was movement. She began to rock herself and work her mittened hands against her knees. It was a job she'd done countless times, sitting at the edge of an ice rink. It distracted and calmed her.

So what kind of gear had Jordy stowed in this thing, anyway?

She climbed into the rear, found a green nylon duffel bag in the tail section, dragged it out, and unzipped it. She pulled out something made of crunchy, dark blue nylon—an insulated snowsuit! Then came a large, sinuous maroon mass—a mummy-style sleeping bag. "Oh, my God, am I glad to see these!" she said aloud, hugging their slithery bulk to herself. Her breath steamed in front of her.

A survival kit. Willa looked out at the chasing, rumbling storm and imagined it a hundred miles deep in every direction. She cleared her throat.

Reaching back into the green duffel bag, she pulled out a small camp stove, two metal canisters of fuel, and a single-blade ax. Good, good. Next she hauled out a rattling stainless-steel mess kit, a blue plastic tarp that crackled in the cold, three skeins of nylon cord, and a couple of signal flares. All good. So she could cook, but was there any food?

She grabbed a bulging red nylon sack, slipped the stay up the drawcord, and opened it. It held freeze-dried meal packets, a bread bag full of oatmeal, and a small bag containing salt, pepper, and spices. In the bottom of the nylon sack were five dark brown bars wrapped in plastic—Jordy's goat bars! They were his home-made version of energy bars, made from oatmeal, molasses, and various nuts and seeds. They weren't exactly tasty, but at least she wouldn't starve for a few days.

One last small yellow bag contained a multi-tool, a couple of butane lighters, some candles, a small notebook, and a mechanical pencil. Nice! She could write home, put a message in a bottle. She smiled a crooked smile as she stowed everything but the candles in the pockets of her flight suit. The idea of keeping notes for later—yes, there would be a later, a time after all this. Yes!

This was good—she would stay warm; she would sleep and eat.

She tucked the signal flares into a pocket inside her parka and looked out again at the oceanic billows. No point in lighting one now. That would just be a waste. She would wait until she heard a search plane and the spotters could see a flare. She looked at her watch—9:30 a.m.

She had shelter in the plane. Stay with the plane—that was the rule.

Glancing around the cramped cargo hold, she went on with her inventory. A folding stretcher, bound for the nursing station, leaned against the port side. Nearby its cushion was rolled up inside a plastic wrapper. Her duffel bag held personal items. She was wearing longjohns, a flight suit, a parka, and insulated boots. What a camping trip this was going to be.

All right, then. *Calm down*, she told herself.

Willa climbed back into the pilot's seat, unfolded her navigation chart, and tried to work out her position. The chart shook in her hands.

The fact was, she didn't know how far off course the storm had taken her, from what point on her route, or in what direction. She might have drifted to the southeast, since the front had come from the northwest. But sometimes winds blew in different directions at different altitudes, or they could rotate in a big arc.

She would be well overdue in Peawanuck by ten o'clock. Jordy's flight plan would have given his time of departure, which he'd told her was 5:30 a.m., and she had kept to the plan.

She imagined what would happen. They would send search planes out—when the storm let up. They would search her flight path. What else did they have to go by? Jordy's flight plan. Of course, Jordy would tell them too, when he woke up. He'd be the first to know . . .

Doubts and fears crowded in. Even if they had Jordy's flight plan, she could be fifty miles off that path. The wilderness up here was absorbent and unimaginably vast.

Bad headache. She leaned back.

No radio. No radio. No radio. What a mess she had gotten herself into. What was she going to do? She had the two flares. And she could build a fire. Until the storm passed, she had to stew in her own juices.

Fact was, the trips she had taken with Bud and Ray took some of the edge off the terror. They'd gone into the wilderness lake regions of Ontario and Manitoba, both summer and winter. She knew you could stay comfortable winter camping with the proper planning and common sense. She remembered how they listened and watched, talked and sang. Bud played his harmonica around the fire at night.

Willa pulled her harmonica out of an inner pocket and fingered it, thinking about Bud. She wasn't in the mood to play, but it brought back earlier times when Bud sat across a fire from her and Ray.

Ray. *Help me, Ray.*

She remembered her thermos of tea and poured the last cup into her travel mug. It was jasmine tea, barely lukewarm now, but fragrant and comforting. She looked out the window and wondered how long it would take them to find her.

Would they see her? They could pass within a quarter of a mile and never see a thing. If trees and long shadows hid her, the spotters would see nothing. At high noon in mid-January at this latitude the sun rose less than twenty degrees above the horizon. The shadow of a tree would be more than three times its height.

Willa studied the chart and tried to think. Where was she when she lost her bearings, how much time elapsed before she landed, and where might she have come down? She had little idea of the speed and direction of the wind after she entered the storm. The uncertainties left her with an area a hundred miles long and—who knew?—sixty? a hundred? miles wide.

The region was a maze of countless thousands of rivers, lakes, and bogs. No feature was distinctive enough to be identified on the ground by a stranger with a map. She had no idea which direction from any of the native communities in that region she was. What if they didn't find her? How would she know which way to go?

4

What to Do

As a student pilot Willa had taken a ground-school course that covered emergencies. Jordy had talked about the subject too. One thing she recalled was that you could burn engine oil to create smoke.

The temperature was dropping fast. She had better drain the oil now, before it turned to jelly. She opened the mess kit and emptied the contents of the large outer kettle back into the bag so she'd have a container.

Stepping out the right door into the snow, Willa turned her back to the wind. She ducked under and crawled over the low-hanging branches that clutched the nose of the plane, and worked her way to the left side of the engine.

But the kettle would stay clean. A tree limb had smashed the cowling and punched the engine, letting all the oil drain out. "A fine mess," she muttered, looking at the molasses-colored streaks down below.

Her mind set on making smoke, she looked into the plane through the windshield, and her eyes fell on the seats. The vinyl upholstery and foam rubber cushions would do it.

When Willa left that morning the temperature had been a mild zero degrees Fahrenheit in Sioux Lookout. The cold front had dropped the mercury far below that. She tightened her hood and looked around at the trees. Her eyes watered from the cold. She needed to gather branches for a fire, the dead branches near the bottom of the tree trunks. Snow covered everything on the ground.

Little new snow was falling now, but the wind blew schooners across the lake, and wails both low and high arose as if from a cello of the gods. Standing safe beside the plane, Willa let the snow grains bite into her cheeks for a few moments. The temperature was at least 15 below—she could tell from the way the air singed her nostrils when she inhaled. Yet compared to the overwhelming isolation, the cold was nothing.

She had to pee. She started to move away from the plane but realized immediately that she could not simply walk off through the snow. It was too deep. She worked her way to the other side of the big black spruce at the nose of the plane and crawled under the limbs. There was just enough room to crouch in the hollow underneath.

Turquoise and gold flashed from the Knights hockey team emblem on her zipper tab. She had to shuck her parka in order to get far enough out of the flight suit to squat. She drilled a dark, steaming hole in the snow. A relief, but the cold was torture. She snapped back into the top of her flight suit and jerked the parka back on. Shivers. What a hassle just to pee. She wished she had a pair of windproof pants instead of the flight suit. But the wind found every crack; the fewer the seams, the better.

Crawling out from the hollow, she looked back at the pit beneath the lower branches. Not all spruces were so accommodating. Most stood like ragged bottle brushes, sheltering nothing but the bugs in their bark.

Remembering that she needed wood for a fire, she trudged laboriously around the nearest spruces, breaking dead sticks and branches off and piling them near the plane. No use trying to build a fire now; the smoke would only hide in the streaming snow.

She couldn't collect wood for long. After half an hour she was worn out from the wind, and her legs and face were freezing. She returned to the plane, climbed into the co-pilot's seat, and slammed the door behind her. Out of the wind. She lay back in her seat and nodded into blankness. After a spell she woke and rummaged through her duffel bag to find her field thermometer. She unscrewed it from its tube and set it on the dash above the instrument panel. Ten minutes later she checked it: 18 below zero.

Willa squeezed her mittened hands between her thighs and shook her head in her parka hood. No one knew where she was. *She* didn't know where she was.

She battled a silent whirlpool. *Calm, focus, think*, she counseled herself. She sat for a long time with her eyes closed, shivering as much from panic as from cold. A branch squeaked against the windshield.

There would be no heat out here. None. Her own body would be her heater. The camp stove—it would heat food and water. A campfire wasn't much good for warming yourself in the winter, unless you got wet and needed to dry out. You could warm your fingers and feet if you were careful. If you were not—she recalled the acrid smell of scorched nylon.

The sun would warm the day some. Its light, short-lived though it would be, was the greater comfort in winter. Body heat was the key. In the mummy bag she'd be able to sleep in fairly wicked cold, if she stayed out of the wind. Bud's iron-clad rule: keep moving, stay dry, don't work up a sweat.

Daylight fell into the afternoon. When was sunset? About four, maybe four-fifteen. Total darkness would settle in by five o'clock. The wind had grown razor-sharp. Out on the lake, snow plumes snaked away to the southeast. Willa turned her face down into the neck of her parka and breathed the warm air inside.

Hungry.

She put on her light gloves in place of the mittens and clambered into the rear. She pawed through the survival kit and pulled out a dinner packet. Water, she needed water. Taking the big kettle, she pushed the door open, scooped the pot full of snow, and slammed the door shut again. She crawled back into the rear and unpacked the camp stove, screwed it together, and pumped it. She snapped the butane lighter again and again. It gave great sparks, but it wouldn't light. She got angry and squeezed it in her fist. Then she tried it again, and it jazzed to flame. It had just needed warming up. But then the stove wouldn't light. Damn! Nothing worked! Wait—was the fuel too cold?

She tucked the frigid stove and fuel bottle inside her parka to warm them. The cold metal of the stove stole heat from her body and made her shake. She rocked herself, squeezed her arms and legs together, wrestled herself for heat.

Twenty minutes later, she got the stove started and put the kettle of snow on it. The fierce, torch-like flame took a fair time to turn the plug of snow into half an inch of water. She leaned out and scooped up more snow in another pot and added that to the kettle on the stove. Once a little water had pooled in the bottom, the melting went faster.

From the past came Bud's voice advising her on one of their winter trips: *Always get ice to melt for water, if you can; it melts faster than snow. Snow traps air and insulates itself, takes longer to melt down.* To get ice, though, she'd have to wade through heavy drifts to the lake, dig out a hole to the ice, chip out some shards with the ax, and then wade back. She would melt snow for now. Besides, she had no shovel. How would she dig through three feet of snow?

Darkness had fallen by the time Willa had enough water boiling in the pot to cook the freeze-dried dinner mix. She emptied a packet into the pot, tapping a finger against the packet to make sure the mix was all in, and put the lid on. She lit a candle. The flickering glow filled the tiny cabin. A bucket of tension left her shoulders as she caught the aroma of the meal cooking.

Willa flattened the crinkly foil packet over her thigh. Beef Basil Rotini. Just the food for a disaster! When it had swelled up in the pot, she dug into the steaming meal with the one spoon she had from the kit. Each mouthful of the chunks of meat, chewy pasta, and fragrant herbs calmed her stomach and lifted her spirits. Amazing how good the stuff tasted after a plane crash. She snorted and nearly choked.

The windows had grown white with frost from her cooking, and her breath issued in clouds. Willa scraped the inside of the stainless-steel kettle to get out the last morsels of stew, now grown cold. The coating that remained inside was already freezing. Willa gave up trying to clean the pot further.

"I don't think we have a bacteria problem here," she said, watching the words echo down a school hall and arrange themselves in the yearbook beside her outdated photo. The reverie faded; her fingers were growing numb in the light gloves. She slipped her heavy mitts back on.

Inside the metal plane Willa was protected from the wind but could not move around much. The cold was relentless. She changed into the snowsuit. It was large on her, but she felt almost instantly warmer.

Deeply exhausted and clumsier by the minute, she pushed boxes into the front and to the side, unfolded the stretcher, and laid out the cushion. It resembled a narrow chaise longue, barely fitting lengthwise into the hold. She unpacked the mummy bag, put it on the stretcher, and lay down on it. Tired, dizzy tired—she hadn't slept much the night before. By now it was 6:30, totally dark. She took off her parka and boots and then slipped her felt boot liners back on. She slid into the bag, zipped herself in, and blew out the candle.

"Here I am, lolling on the beach in sunny Ontario," she slurred amid waves of fatigue. The headache had gone. Sparks flew about on the black screen of her eyelids as she sank into the cot. Tomorrow, tomorrow they would come. A plane would land nearby, taxi up to her . . .

Inside the wingless, legless airplane, wrapped in darkness, she hurtled through space. She heard clicks and creaks as the wind worked at the plane's rudder and the branch rubbed against the windshield. Once she heard a sharp *boom* that ran right through the ground, and she knew it for what it was—lake ice splitting in the intense cold.

Several times Willa fell out of the hammock of sleep as the cold air burned her nostrils. She finally unzipped far enough to reach into her duffel bag and pull out a knit cap. She tucked it into the mummy-bag hood over her mouth and nose, then sagged back into a restless sleep.

Twice during the night she woke up chilled. The first time she stretched and tensed herself until she warmed up, and dropped back off. The second time she awoke, the cold was so intense that it frightened her. She opened the bag, put on her parka over the snowsuit, and drew the hood down to her eyebrows. She slapped the stocking cap on the edge of the stretcher to beat off the frost from her breath, replaced it over her face, and zipped back up inside the bag. She did not wake again until first light.

5

Hope for Rescue

When Willa opened her eyes, dim blue light defined the windows. She was unsurprised at where she was; it was as if she hadn't slept. Frost bristled from the stocking cap and the parka hood. With a little flexing she stayed warm inside the bag, but the temperature was monstrous cold, worse than she'd ever experienced before.

Her breath floated up like puffs of talcum powder. She envisioned the desolation—the plane like a dismembered insect, the frozen waste, the jagged wind. She closed her eyes against it and turned her head to bury her face in the warm mummy hood. No, no . . . It had to be a bad dream . . .

Ray! Willa! Up 'n' at 'em! Daylight in the swamp! Bud's voice had called up the stairs, rousting them out of bed for a ski trip.

Willa opened her eyes. Her stomach was knotted. She thought of search planes and rose up on her elbow. Aach! Her neck and shoulders hurt! She looked at her watch—7:30—and the sun wasn't even up. The planes couldn't be out yet. She had time to make some hot tea.

She unzipped the bag far enough to reach out and grab the stove. Cradling the stove and fuel bottle inside the sleeping bag, she remembered seeing a bag of oatmeal in the survival kit. That would be good too, hot oatmeal. Her belly growled.

Willa loosened the drawstring of her hood, pulled off the encrusted stocking cap, and slapped it against the wall. The air was almost too cold to breathe. It was frying her nostrils. She put the cap back over her mouth and nose, tucking it into the hood. She could still feel the burn of the frigid metal stove through her leather gloves.

She dozed again. When she woke, she unzipped her parka and put the stove inside it, nearer her body. It was still too cold to hold it inside her snowsuit. She checked her watch and waited another fifteen minutes. She pumped the fuel bottle inside the sleeping bag. She waited a while longer, cradling the stove closely, then threw the bag off and immediately lit the stove. It sputtered, hesitated, bloomed with a lazy yellow flame, and sputtered some more. At last it began a loud, husky hissing and the flame turned blue and strong. She felt the heat on her face as she pulled on her stiff boots. She needed to move, to warm up.

While the pot of snow was melting, Willa stepped out the door. It was strange to climb out without a wing overhead. Blown snow had nearly filled in the pit she'd made yesterday. She trampled down a small area, jumping up and down and flapping her arms to get her circulation going.

Within half a minute she had to stop and cover her face with her mitts. She gazed on the maimed airplane, up to the snow-mantled trees, and then out across the lake. She felt as if she were looking over the edge of a cliff—only she'd already fallen. If nobody came for her, she'd hit bottom. Her mouth was dry.

The light breeze and caustic cold chased her back inside. She stared at her thermometer—43 degrees below zero. She'd heard at times on the morning weather report that the temperature had fallen that low overnight, but she'd never been out in it.

Breathing and heating water had generated frost that clung in tiny florets to the windows and the ceiling of the cabin. At 43 below, a mild wind would burn exposed flesh in seconds.

Willa sat on the stretcher, sipped her tea, ate hot oatmeal, and allowed the steam to bathe her face. The warmth brought calm. The panic of waking up in a plane wreck at 43 below loosened its grip. Her whirling thoughts began to settle.

Where was she? Could they see her? Hell—the plane was half under the trees and the rest was in the shadows. The rescue pilots would never see her. She'd have to flag them down or catch them with a flare or something.

She had an urge to run outside and scan the sky. But the breeze was like shark's teeth. She hung her head. Who knew—days might pass before they flew over.

She scraped a patch of frost off the window and looked out toward the lake. The wind was calmer; the sky was clear. Maybe she could get a smoky fire going. An orange glow rose behind the trees. Maybe the sun would warm things up a little. She downed the last of her tea, gone cold now.

Suddenly a distant hum—an airplane! She bolted for the door, flew outside, and churned into the snow, fumbling for a flare. With her second and third steps her legs plunged deep into the light, powdery drift and she fell forward. Her arms drove into the suffocating depths as snow stung her face.

She sputtered and shook her head, twisted and struggled in outrageous slow motion. Looking up, she screamed, "Down here!

Here! Here! *Hey!*" She fought to wave her arms but couldn't raise herself up. She kicked and crawled and flailed . . . and the drone wandered slowly away. Finally she saw it, a glinting speck disappearing to the southwest.

Willa went limp in the mushy hole she'd thrashed in the snow, gasping for air as she shielded her face with her mitts. Gone! They'd missed her! But they were looking! They were looking! She was crushed and elated all at once.

Ah, but the air was needles, rasping like crushed glass into her lungs, making her cough. She had to get back inside.

Floundering in powder, her feet squeaking and crunching in the muffled depths, she lurched back to the pit next to the plane. She trembled from exertion and shock. Panting through her mitts, she scanned the empty and soundless sky. God, her face burned! In one motion she opened the door and sat down in the right seat, latching the door closed again.

In those few minutes her face had grown numb. She slung away her mitts, pulled off her gloves, and cupped her face in her bare hands. They had missed her! They had missed her! The silence, the emptiness, was cruel. Her heart drummed in her chest.

Rubbing her face, she had a fleeting memory of a pickup game of hockey on a bitter cold day. The other kids—all boys—ignored her. She'd been allowed in the game because they needed an extra player to even up the two sides . . .

The cold nipped her knuckles. She put her soft gloves on, cupped her face again. Tears threatened.

. . . And then Ray had intercepted and passed the puck to

her. She'd raced off so hard—*Go for it, Woolly!* yelled Ray. She skated furiously toward the goal markers, amid screams and cheers, then slipped and hit the ice, a sprawling starfish growling along the pitted surface as the scuffing rumble knifed by her. She didn't touch the puck again that game, but the cheers rang in her dreams for a long time.

"They'll be back." Willa said it like Ray, tough, cocksure. She was still breathing hard, covering her face with the stocking cap. She'd broken a sweat in her struggle in the snow. She unzipped her parka and the snowsuit partway to vent vapor.

She needed snowshoes—couldn't move around out here without them. She had to watch out and not be sweating. The water vapor from her body would freeze in her clothing so that it wouldn't trap heat any longer. She would get cold, risk hypothermia. She drew the parka hood up loosely, tucked the stocking cap back over her face, and zipped back up.

Snowshoes. Why were there none in the survival pack? Without snowshoes she couldn't get out in the clear to signal, couldn't run with a flare. She could build a fire, but unless she could move around freely she couldn't gather enough wood to keep it going.

She had gathered a bundle of branches, but they wouldn't burn for long. The fire would have to be built on the spot at the first sound of a plane. A wild thought came to her. Maybe she could set one of the trees on fire! Was there any fuel left in the wing tanks? She'd find a bucket and check.

In the cargo area, among the boxes of supplies headed for the nursing station in Peawanuck, Willa found a large plastic bucket labeled PARADINE, a disinfectant hand soap. She zipped up her parka and pulled on her mitts, then took the heavy bucket outside and unscrewed the cap on the spout. But the contents had solidified in the cold. After a long struggle with a screwdriver from the Cessna's toolkit, she got the entire lid off and dumped the gelatinous, pale green plug in the snow. Patiently she worked her way to the wings. Their straight contours were visible through the top blanket of new snow, only ten or fifteen yards behind the plane.

The tanks had ruptured—that was no surprise. The left wing tank was completely split open and dry. The right wing had hit a cluster of small aspen saplings, which caused less damage. Moving slowly and awkwardly around to the right wing, she scooped away snow with the bucket and positioned it under the tear. Then she climbed carefully onto the wing, walked in a crouch to its tip, and jumped off the end into the snow. By lifting and twisting the end of the wing, she was able to catch about half a gallon of fuel.

She looked at the clear liquid in the bucket. Wait—this stuff might work in the camp stove too. Should she save it for the stove or use it to start a signal fire?

Burn it. Now would be the time of the most intense searching. Willa pressed the lid on the bucket and looked around for a tree. She picked a spruce some thirty yards away from the plane and slowly worked her way to it, plunging her legs down again and again to trample a pathway and resting occasionally to avoid sweating.

Once she had made a path, she moved the dry branches she'd gathered the night before and piled them against the base of the tree. She set the fuel bucket beside the pile. When the next plane approached, she would sprint to the tree and set the fire.

The cold was too severe for her to stand around outside. Willa stepped back into the plane, sat down, and gazed out at the dark trees with their snowy shoulders set against the deep blue of the winter sky.

She could just hear Bud's bloody lecture. IT IS YOUR RESPONSIBILITY to check the emergency locator transmitter. WHAT WERE YOU THINKING OF when you took off like that . . . What gave you the RIGHT . . . Who gave you PERMISSION . . . How could you just TAKE OFF with your uncle's airplane . . . YOU SMASHED AN AIRPLANE . . . You might have been KILLED . . .

Willa slumped against the seat. *Never mind. Never mind. I can fix it. I can fix it . . .*

She pondered how to make snowshoes. She needed a frame with some type of webbing, a big footprint to spread her weight out on the snow. Bindings of some kind to attach the frames to her boots.

Most wood-frame snowshoes were made of a single strip of wood bent into a teardrop shape. The wood had to be steamed. She couldn't do that out here. But she'd seen a pair of snowshoes once, on a wall in a lodge, that were pointed in front and back, like a canoe. Yes—on the trip to Churchill with Bud. Two pieces had been joined in front and back, spread apart by ribs.

So—bind a pair of green branches together at both ends. Spread the branches apart with a crosswise rib. The rib would make a platform for the bindings, to fasten the whole thing to her foot. The nylon cord from the survival kit could form the webbing.

The idea blazed in her brain. She could do this! The next plane wouldn't catch her wallowing in the drifts.

By 10:30 a.m. the temperature had climbed to minus 34 and Willa had warmed herself with another mug of hot tea. She had thought through her scheme as far as she could without getting her hands on the sticks. She would make up the rest as she went along.

Picking up the single-blade ax from the survival kit, she stepped out of the plane. She moved slowly from tree to tree in the spruce grove, looking on the lower trunks for green, pliable branches with the right thickness and length.

Within twenty minutes she had found two and was moving patiently from one spruce to another searching for a third bough. As she quietly scanned a tree, out of the corner of her eye she caught sight of a large white hare. She turned slow as a minute hand to see better between the branches.

The hare was plump and bright-eyed. It must have found plenty to eat. Swiveling its long ears, the hare rose up on its haunches and sniffed the air with a tender, mobile nose. Then came a sudden puff of snow and the creature was gone.

Willa must have spooked it—so vulnerable, yet at home here.

By the time Willa found the fourth branch, it was near noon, and the temperature had risen to 28 below zero. The day turned out calm and bright. With all her activity, the stocking cap, riddled with frost, kept pulling out. She tied it in place with her bandana. She waggled her chin and squinched her cheeks to chase the numbness away.

She was ready for some hot soup. She examined the four spruce branches, each close to five feet long, and then cut another branch, remembering that she needed some sticks for cross braces.

She turned toward the crippled plane. It looked like a grass-hopper with its wings folded. She began slowly punching a trail back toward it, thinking of the times she had collected grasshop-pers and other insects with her mother.

Then—the drone of another plane! While collecting wood she had worked her way fifty or sixty yards to the other side of the Cessna from the torch tree. Her roundabout path was twice that distance. Too far!

Electrified, she dropped the branches, pulled a flare out of her parka, lit it, and looked frantically to see which way to run to get in the plane's line of sight. The sound was to the east. She tried to make her way to the lake, but she bogged down again; the snow was as deep as ever. She could not fly over it. She was imprisoned, marooned on a tiny island in an ocean of snow.

As Willa struggled to make headway, holding the flare aloft, the seconds raced by . . . and the sound faded. She dropped to her knees, unbelieving. The flare sputtered a pale pink against the bright snow.

"Over here! Come back! Come back!" she screamed. She rose up and threw the flare in the direction of the plane's dying murmur as hard as she could. Why had she lit the thing? She should have waited! Now there was just one left.

Two planes! How many times would they fly over here? Two planes, neither very close. It wasn't good. Missed twice.

Willa stared out across the spruce tops into the deep blue,

spiraling into an airless funk. Shouldn't have gotten so far from the burn tree. Shouldn't have lit the flare . . . *Idiot!*

The weight came down, a sickening sense of defeat and panic. Two planes had missed her. That had to be all. How could there be any more? She stood swaying in her tracks, black spots swirling in the air around her.

All right, get over it. What would her big brother think? Ray wouldn't be mean, he'd just say, *C'mon, Woolly, let's go.*

Maybe she would just sit and make ice. Tears bathed her face. She pressed her mitts to her cheeks and staggered toward the plane.

She threw the spruce branches down and stumbled inside, collapsing in the co-pilot's seat. There she wept, the tears stinging her face until the iciness forced her to wipe them away with her mitts. She climbed into the rear and lay down on the stretcher, sobbing like an abandoned child.

Finally the cold goaded her into the sleeping bag, where she snuffled and shook, dimly expecting to lie there until she died. She didn't even bother to kick her boots off. She fell into a pit, a darkness like an eclipse, all light and hope extinguished. She lay there for hours.

She dreamed of Bud, years back, stopped on his skis at the bottom of a long hill. She'd wiped out and was struggling to get back up. He was summoning her on with a wave of his arm. *C'mon, Tiger!*

Another dream. Her mother was carrying her into the house. She'd fallen on the ground, trying to get into a hammock. The darn thing had just dumped her out. *There, there, honey, I know it hurts. You got the breath knocked out of you. It'll be all right.*

She woke up shivering, her sleeping-bag hood an icy mess around her face.

Damn, she was still alive.

C'mon, Tiger! It'll be all right, honey. Go for it, Woolly! They were teaming up on her.

Willa rubbed her face with her bare hands and sat up. Maybe she should give it another shot. Give it another shot.

6

A Way Will Open

There could be another flyover; it could happen, it could happen. She would need the snowshoes then. What else did she have to do? Might as well get ready.

Willa retrieved the spruce branches, sat down on the stretcher, and pulled out the knife blade on her multi-tool. She trimmed the branches and cut them down to about four and a half feet, letting the chips fall at her feet. The large ends were quite a bit stouter than the small ends. She decided to mate the same-size ends so that the snowshoes would be symmetrical from side to side.

With nylon cord from the survival kit, she bound a pair of branches together at each end. Then she pulled the branches about a foot apart in the middle, where she intended to tie a rib—rats! One branch had broken under the strain. So spruce wouldn't work. Too brittle. She broke the other sticks over her knee and threw them into the front of the plane. A couple of hours wasted.

Frowning, Willa put a pot of snow on the stove to make some soup. She lit a long slice from one of the spruce branches in the flame and enjoyed the smell as it burned.

Finally the soup was hot. Oh, it was good! And the warmth of the stove and the heat of the pot were welcome to her hands, aching with cold. Inside the plane the air was still colder than 20 below zero, and gripping the knife and the sticks had cut down circulation in her fingers. She put her mitts back on over her gloves.

All right, if not spruce, what? There was plenty of aspen. A stand of saplings grew right at the edge of the lake. Taking the ax with her, she trudged slowly out to the leafless grove and cut a five-foot section from a slender young trunk. She bent it around her knee to test it. It was like rubber! Good. With more barging, punching, leaning, and dragging, Willa moved around to chop off three more five-foot lengths, plus some extra for the ribs.

Back in the plane, Willa sat down on the stretcher with the branches and made them smooth, cutting off all the twigs and bark. Her breath got in the way of seeing, so she exhaled from the side of her mouth. The stretcher creaked and the nylon shell of her clothing rustled. Her knife talked with the wood in scrapes and clicks.

She carved a shallow groove around the circumference of each branch a couple of inches from the end. Then she bound the long frame pieces together in pairs, as she had before, tying the joints tightly with nylon cord from the kit. She hummed as she cut two ribs and bound one across the center of each frame, spreading the frame into a canoe-like shape. At each joint tied with nylon cord, she cut grooves so she could recess the cord below the surface of the wood and help keep it in place.

But her fingers grew very cold—much of the work had to be done with bare hands. Every few minutes Willa had to stop and hold her numb fingers against her cheeks or put on her mitts and let her hands warm up. From time to time she grew chilled all over; then she had to step outside and dance and stretch to get her blood going again.

After switching back to her light gloves, she tied the cord from the spool at the end of one of the frames and began wrapping the cord tightly around the frame. But that wouldn't work; surely it would slip unless she anchored it better. She unwound the cord and tried wrapping it around the frame piece on each side once before drawing it across to the other side. That looked better. She wrapped cord around and around, from side to side, spacing the turns a thumb's width apart.

Dusk had set in by the time she took the snowshoes outside and, placing the ball of each foot upon a rib, lashed them onto her boots.

She lifted her right foot high and stepped out of the packed area by the door into deeper snow. But when she lifted her left foot, the tip caught in the snow, sending her into a short dive. She rolled over in the drift and wiped the snow out of her face. "Come on in, the water's fine!" she called out, lying limp for a moment.

"Just a little crunchy," she muttered as she got back onto her feet. She swatted the snow from her clothes and carefully stepped forward again. The snowshoes did support her; she sank less than a foot with each step. But the front tips dropped when she lifted her feet.

Of course—she'd put the heavy ends in front! On her lap in the Cessna they looked all right. But she wasn't building a pair of barges. She wanted to push as little snow around as possible. She wanted to walk on top of it. Web feet, web walkers. The front ends needed to be lighter than the back ends.

And the webbing she had strung, wrapped over and under the frame in a double layer, trapped snow—that made the snowshoes heavier. Soon the outside joint of the rib on the left snowshoe began slipping. The webbing was coming loose.

There was no help for it—the job needed more care. She went back inside, lit a candle, and took the snowshoes completely apart. She whittled the ends of the frame pieces flat where they overlapped, and this time she used fishline from the kit to bind the joints tightly.

She notched each rib carefully into the frame pieces so that the rib itself would hold the sides apart and the fishline binding the joints needn't bear all the stress. This time the thicker, heavier ends of the frame pieces would form the tail. When she lifted her foot, the tail would drop; the nose would rise. Then she could stride across the snow.

It took more bare fingers. She couldn't work long before needing to plunge hands into mitts or into her hair in the parka hood. Her materials were as cold as the air, colder than 20 degrees below zero. A couple of times, as she massaged her scalp to warm her fingers, fear raced up her spine. The pilots had already flown over this area twice . . .

But they might fly over again, and the snowshoes would save her. With them Willa could run into the open with a flare, and she could build fires. The work kept her spirits up.

The webbing had to be done differently. There had to be one flat layer of webbing, only one. Maybe she could string the cord through holes in the frame, as on a tennis racket. But boring the first hole with the stubby awl on her multi-tool took forever. There were too many holes for that.

Instead, she ringed the frame every inch or so with a groove, and strung cord around the inside, looping it around the frame in each groove and slipping the lead end behind the loop as she took it to the next groove. Bud had taught her about hitches and half hitches, but she wasn't sure which these were. For the webbing, she strung cord from side to side, catching the perimeter line between each pair of grooves. In front of the crosspiece she left a space for her toe to dip through.

By the time Willa was finished stringing the cord, her watch showed nearly 5:00 p.m. and it was far too dark to do such close work. She didn't want to stop, but she was hungry and cold. She warmed the stove inside her parka, then fired it up and put on a pot of snow for her supper.

What would it be tonight? She pawed through the freeze-dried packets and picked out Turkey Teriyaki. "What, no freeze-dried wine?" she said aloud as she warmed her throbbing fingers over the stove. Snowshoes! She could hardly wait to try them.

In the dim light from the stove she wove slender green sticks lengthwise through the segments of zigzagging cord and anchored them with fishline, filling in the meshwork. As the little stove roared and her cooking supper filled the cabin with the smell of turkey and herbs, Willa finished the webbing. She propped the snowshoes against the cabin wall. She'd try them first thing in the morning. Supper was almost ready. Her appetite roared with the stove.

Each meal packet was supposed to serve two, according to the label, but she had eaten the entire meal the first night and expected to have no problem tonight, ravenous as she was. When the Turkey Teriyaki was done, she set it aside and immediately put on another pot of snow. She picked up the steaming stew and slurped it down, spoonful after spoonful. She finished it well before there was enough hot water for tea, so she picked up one of the cardboard boxes of supplies the plane had been carrying and took a look.

The box wasn't labeled, except with the name of the nursing station at Peawanuck. She cut it open with her knife and found three smaller boxes with various pharmaceuticals. Cefachlor. Augmentin. Betamethasone dipropionate. She shoved the box under the stretcher and opened another. It contained more medicines. God, she hoped nobody in the village would suffer for her mistake!

She opened more boxes—rubber gloves, splints, bandages, syringes, tape, scissors and other instruments, record books. She threw a pair of scissors and a couple of rolls of surgical tape into her duffel bag, along with cotton pads she could use for toilet paper.

When the water was ready, she made some tea and filled her thermos bottle. She left the pot half full of water and shut off the stove. The water would freeze in the pot and be ready for remelting in the morning. *For you, Bud,* she thought. Ice that would melt faster than snow. She wrapped her thermos of hot water in the hood of the mummy bag, hoping the warmth would drive off some of the tear-slush. What a funny thing—tears didn't freeze like plain water.

She was seized with a strange hysterical laugh that broke into tears, which caused more laughter. But then she was calm. She talked silently.

What's happening is happening. Here is where I am. I am all right. This is just a nice little camping trip. It's survivor school, eh? Me, I'm a survivor, right? Just get up and go again. Did you ever get knocked down as many times as I have, Ray? Never mind, brother. You stood up for me plenty.

As Willa's mug of tea steamed on a box by her knee, she continued opening cartons. One contained plastic bags of intravenous fluids that were frozen solid. Would the saline solutions be okay to cook food in? She grimaced. Melted snow seemed preferable.

But how about the bottles of alcohol—would they be useful? Maybe she could make a lamp that would burn alcohol. She wasn't sure whether it would work in the stove.

She looked at the bottles more carefully. One hundred percent ethyl alcohol. Removing a cap, she sniffed. Yeah. She'd had a small glass of wine a few times in the last couple of years, at family celebrations. But it touched painful wounds, that odor. Why had Bud drunk before he quit? Why did Jordy drink?

She downed the last of her tea, then fished out her flashlight and read her thermometer: 24 below. Sitting on the stretcher, she looked at her snowshoes. She was tired, dead tired. Eight o'clock seemed absurdly early, but she was past ready to bed down, to sleep, to escape the demons of fear and loneliness that were closing in.

Ice was still embedded in the mummy-bag hood; she'd better

wear the parka to bed. A little ice remained in the parka hood, but not as much as before.

In the bag she stretched and shivered, pressed her cold hands together between her thighs, and pumped the muscles of her arms and shoulders and thighs for warmth. She rocked herself, heard the rustle of the bag and the creak of the stretcher frame, imagined search-and-rescue planes, and fell asleep.

7

Snow Walkers

In the blue light before sunrise, Willa drank the last of her tea while it was still hot. Quiet sat like a bell jar over the world. The stove ticked. Willa pondered. She began trembling. She could not match the massive cold and emptiness. There was no help, no life support.

She screwed the stopper on her thermos and checked her thermometer: 18 below.

That was a big jump. Maybe she could last another day or two, eh?

The snowshoes caught her eye and shouted, *Walk!* She snatched them up, binding laces dangling, and stepped outside. No, she couldn't match it all at once, but maybe she could take it on little by little.

In the pit beside the door she placed her feet on the snowshoe ribs and tied them to her boots with nylon cord. Then she walked out into the deep snow.

They worked! They worked like proper snowshoes. She allowed herself some cautious excitement. The back ends dropped with each step. The snowshoes were a little heavy, but they felt sturdy, and her feet sank only about ten inches. She felt as if she were walking on water.

She toured the site gingerly, keeping an eye on the snow-shoes to make sure they weren't coming apart again. Her spirits lifted with each stride. Then she broke into a waddling jog. She whooped and lifted her arms to the spruces. Prancing about, feeling downright giddy, she launched into a childhood song about waltzing with bears. She bounded around on the snow, freed now from its strangling entrapments.

After a few minutes she stopped, wary of working up a sweat. She stood still, opened her parka, and unzipped the top of her snowsuit to ventilate for a minute. As her breathing slowed, Willa looked up, closed her eyes, and cackled in gratitude. Thank God, thank God! Nothing like a little waltz in the woods at dawn. Snowshoes!

The only thing that bothered her was the bindings. The cord just didn't work very well; it let the snowshoes twist too much on her feet. If only she had some lamp wick or belt webbing. The seatbelts! The nylon straps were strong and lightweight—perfect for the job. It didn't take long to free them from the plane. "Fasten your seatbelts," she said as she tied the snowshoes to her feet with the new bindings.

Wearing her new snow walkers, Willa set about gathering more dry branches for a signal fire. The sun was just chinning the trees, and the sky was clear. She broke a couple of dry branches off one tree and was moving toward another when she heard a sound like a buzzing mosquito. Another plane! Out to the west!

She scuttled to the fire spruce and tried to sight the plane. It was hidden behind the trees, but the time had to be now, before it passed her by. She pulled the lid off the bucket and soaked the pile of branches with fuel. Then she took one wet branch and stepped back a few paces, lit it, and tossed it toward the pile.

The fuel thumped into flame. The sticks crackled and tendrils of smoke curled through the branches. From a safe distance away, Willa watched, blood thumping in her temples. The tree stood massive as the sticks burned almost unseen beneath its branches.

Time sagged by. She scanned the sky in the west, trying to spot the plane. Setting fire to a tree was as slow as melting snow! The fuel burned off and the blaze fell back, working to get a grip on the sticks. Puffs of steam seeped from the branches.

Suddenly there was a rustle up above; Willa followed the sound with her eyes. Her spirits dropped as she saw snow on the tree falling down from the middle, then from beneath, each cascade touching off the snow below it. Finally a mass fell with a soft whoosh into the burning pile of sticks.

A pale cloud of steam rose.

"No-o-o-o!" yelled Willa, arching in agony. Oh, God. She turned and ran back toward the lake as fast as she could move on the snowshoes. If only she could get into the open . . . But when she stopped forty yards out onto the lake, the sound had stopped. The plane was gone.

"Damn! Damn! *Damn!*" she screamed. Her lungs heaved, and her teeth clenched in anger and panic. Not again! Tilting her head back, she squeezed her eyes shut and made a low sound like a cat growling, then dropped down into the snow.

She lay inert on her stomach with her face turned to the left, as she had once lain in Grandma Kucera's patchwork feather bed when she was little and Grandma was very old. Used to be when Willa lay in bed half asleep, she could see patterns slowly rotating, as if her head were inside a giant kaleidoscope filled with patches of cloth. She hadn't seen them for a long time.

When her body hit the snow, her hooded head had pressed out a cavity that gave her air. The snow that clung to her face melted; though it was cold, it wouldn't freeze her skin. She lay in her torpor, watching the navy blue replace corduroy, the rosebud and print being brought on, then a green plaid coming around, followed by the wild goose pillow ticking and the black and white houndstooth . . . *Goose egg.* Ray's voice. Jean holding an ice bag on her head. Hockey stick had caught her.

Coming to, cold and shivering, Willa pulled her knees up, feet still bound to the cockeyed snowshoes. She ached with being alive, alive to suffer and die. Once again she couldn't manage to just quit breathing.

She had given herself up for dead yesterday. Didn't work. Third time would be the charm. *Don't leave me here like this,* she wailed. She tried to cry but didn't have any tears left. *Just let me die, Lord, let me die.*

"That's crazy!"

She jerked her head up. She'd heard it plain as day. A crow veered away. She pushed her legs out and tried to roll over onto her back. Must have imagined it.

Grunting, Willa struggled to get a leg up and untie her foot, but it was all tangled and had nothing to push against. After several minutes she got a leg free, then the other. She tied the snowshoes back on and stood up.

She shuffled slowly back to the plane, sat down in back, and clumsily made tea again.

Why was she making tea? Because she was cold and thirsty. Why didn't she just kill herself? It was hopeless. She was just going to starve or freeze to death. So they all thought she had been killed. Well, they were right. Pretty soon they would be right.

"That's crazy!"

That raspy, jeering voice again. Was it the crow? Spooky. How could a crow sound like that? She shivered. The tea was almost ready.

Well, she certainly hadn't expected a third pass. But she'd had her snowshoes this time, and if the tree had caught . . . Maybe there was still a little hope. Crazy things could happen, things you couldn't foresee.

She took a sip of the hot liquid. She was exhausted. Just doing simple, basic things was so hard. Three times. Hopeless. The tea quickly cooled. She drained the mug and sat staring at the remains of her snowshoe-making on the floor. She was warm again.

Idly she scraped together a small pile of aspen shavings with her foot, and the thought came: she would build a big bonfire and keep it burning night and day! Now that she had snowshoes, she could get around to gather wood, and she'd keep a blaze going until she was found.

Willa picked out a spot far enough away from the nearest tree to avoid another avalanche but close enough to take advantage of the windbreak. She trampled down the snow and laid down a base of stout branches. After piling on the remains of the sticks that had been buried under the torch tree, she went about with her ax and gathered more. She also gathered some green boughs to lay on top of the flames for smoke.

When she'd collected what she thought was enough sticks and branches to last until mid-afternoon, she tore several of the cardboard supply boxes into strips and built a tinder bundle on the platform. She lit the cardboard. Surprisingly, it resisted burning until she shredded it into finer strips.

At last she succeeded in building a fire, but she had to nurse it carefully. Add cold wood too quickly, it would steal heat too fast to ignite; wait too long and—same thing. There was a tense balance between the fire and the cold, like a tug of war between wily adversaries. The balance was easily tipped, and the young fire would die quickly.

After an hour Willa had a fair burn going. Most of the dry branches she'd gathered were in the fire. She laid on some green boughs to make smoke and went out with her ax to gather more wood. The green boughs made good smoke, but they burned up rapidly. She saw that already she'd have to go farther afield.

When she returned, dragging a large bundle of sticks and branches, the fire had melted a pit in the snow and was suffocating. Willa kicked and trampled pathways radiating from the fire so that air could reach it from the sides. She built the blaze back up and went to the plane for the seat cushions.

She cut the seat cover and the foam rubber from the pilot's seat but left the co-pilot's seat alone for the time being—it was comfortable to sit in when she needed to think. She took the foam rubber and vinyl back to the fire and piled them on. They made a darker smoke than the green boughs did, but not as black as burning engine oil.

It was early afternoon and Willa was very hungry again. Since she already had a fire going, she got the pot from the plane, but the blaze was too hot to get close to—there was the risk that she'd burn her outer clothes, especially because she couldn't feel the heat through them. So Willa cleared a patch of snow a few yards away and built another platform of branches. She took burning sticks from the big fire and got a smaller one going. She cooked a freeze-dried dinner while she tended the larger fire. The foam rubber and vinyl burned; she added green boughs to keep the smoke going.

As soon as she'd eaten, she had to go out again for more wood. Feeding the fire was endless toil. She worked on a deadfall, slowly chewing up the trunk with her ax and dragging the pieces back to the blaze. But she could see that tomorrow she would be forced to range farther out for wood. Eventually she would have to move the fire site.

About three o'clock Willa realized that she had gotten careless and allowed herself to sweat up her inner clothes. The sun would set soon; she had to stop and dry out first.

She fetched her flight suit from the plane and cut three saplings, leaving some branches attached. She tied them together near the top to form a tripod and planted it in the snow as a drying rack.

She hung up her parka inside out, took off her snowsuit, and dressed in her flight suit. She turned the snowsuit inside out and hung it up too. It was still 15 below, but there was little breeze. She could stand fairly near the fire and work air in and out of the flight suit, bellows-like, by pulling and pushing on the front. Eventually her pulse slowed and she began to feel the cold soaking her from the rear. She turned her back to the fire, then her front again, but soon she was just rotating misery. After all the hours she'd spent gathering firewood, she was worn out.

She grabbed the snowsuit and shook it out in front of the fire. Little frost remained in it. The sun had swung close to the horizon and the temperature was falling swiftly. She changed back into the insulated suit.

No more planes had come.

Willa fixed her third evening meal at the fire, to conserve stove fuel, and melted water for her thermos. She walked slowly back to the plane, feeling pure dread. She could not hope they would come again. Why would they again pass over an area where three times they had seen nothing?

Her freeze-dried food supply was dwindling fast. She was eating like a horse. Constant toil, emotional stress, and her body's need for heat energy in the unrelenting cold generated an appetite that demanded two full packets a day, in addition to breakfast.

Willa sat down in the co-pilot's seat, holding her mug of tea in both hands. The twilight ebbed.

She would make an alcohol lamp, like the little lamps they used in chem lab. She moved to the rear and lit a candle. Truth was, any project was a relief. That way she didn't have to think.

She rummaged through the boxes and found a case of plastic specimen jars. She pulled one out, made a hole in the metal lid with her multi-tool punch, and pushed a piece of cotton drawcord from a ditty bag through it for a wick. She filled the jar with alcohol, let the alcohol soak up the wick, and lit the lamp. She blew out the candle and took a sip of warm tea.

The lamp burned with a bluer flame than the candle, threw off a little less light, but enough to see by. She had enjoyed chem lab. She liked making things, mixing things, fixing things.

It was the end of her third day. Willa sat on the edge of the low-slung stretcher, pushing the toes of her boots against the bottom of the cabin wall, jiggling to keep warm. She had to pee again, but she was too tired to go out. Instead she used a small pot from the mess kit and then pushed the right door open and dumped the contents to the side. She returned to the stretcher.

They weren't going to find her. What was she going to do? No way were they coming back over here. She looked up at her reflection in the window, which she'd scraped clear of frost. No point in panic, eh. Of course they would find her. *Calm down, Tiger.*

She was getting kind of low on food, though.

She pulled the survival kit over and counted. Three dinner packets, a soup, and a small package of corned beef. Enough oatmeal for tomorrow morning's breakfast. And five of Uncle Jordy's bitter goat bars.

She was going to run out of food. Jeez.

She would get weak, wouldn't have the energy to keep warm. Probably die of hypothermia before she starved.

She had heard that hypothermia victims often lost their sanity, shed their clothes, and wandered off naked in the snow to lie down and sleep forever.

Yeah, she would go sunbathe on the snow-white sand here in sunny Ontario.

Willa shuddered. No, don't be stupid, she told herself. What if there were a chance? Think. What could she eat in this godforsaken frozen wilderness? She had nothing to hunt with, no rifle. A cartoon-like vision of herself throwing her ax at a crow popped into her mind.

Not that Willa had done much shooting. Bud had given her some basic training with a .22, but she'd had no lasting taste for it.

It would have to be something stealthy or tricky, like a trap. What about a snare? She didn't know how to set one up. That was something native trappers and survivalists knew about. She'd heard stories about people catching rabbits with loops of wire, but she'd never seen it done.

Although the kit held basic items of tackle, fishing with a hook through a hole in the ice wasn't practical. For one thing, she didn't have any bait. Where did those disgusting leeches go in January?

Of course, there *were* fish in the lakes—below several feet of ice. That she knew. Bud used to do some ice fishing when she was little. What a mess it would be, chopping through three feet of ice with the ax, only to find that the fish had gone next door. As if they would wait around until the thudding above had opened a hole in the ice.

On one camping trip Bud talked about a fish trap, an old native method of catching fish. If she could remember how to make one, it might save her life.

It would be illegal, of course. She imagined herself building a trap and pulling it from a hole in the ice, full of fish, and then looking up to see a Mountie standing there frowning at her. "I'm afraid you'll have to come with me, ma'am," he'd say.

She began to giggle uncontrollably. "Take me right to jail, sir," she squeaked, holding out a limp wrist and shaking with laughter.

She wiped the tears from her face, snuffled, and heaved a deep sigh.

She was going crazy. She was *not* going crazy. Three days. They wouldn't give up this soon. Would they? But they had been through here three times . . .

Willa was sure that the search would be conducted in a methodical way, that it would have some rationality to it, that she couldn't expect another pass, even if it was theoretically possible.

She would not sit around here day after day until she froze to death. If the planes stopped coming, she would tie on her snowshoes and start walking. Of course, with no food, she would die anyway.

Elementary. She rubbed her mitts on her knees.

She would rather die trying to walk out than sit here like a ninny. But if she could make a fish trap, maybe she could catch enough fish to feed herself for a few days.

If she could make a fish trap.

And if she had some ham, she could make a ham sandwich, if she had some bread.

A fish trap. She looked through her reflection in the window into the darkness.

As they took a breather once at a portage, Bud had explained how nets and fish traps were used by native people in the old days. The women made them. The traps were basically baskets constructed from flexible materials such as vines, roots, and slender branches. Some of them were made to hang in narrow streams. They had a wide mouth, like a horn, and then they skinnied down into a cone or a sock-shaped appendix. Ray had built a little one out of sticks and fishline. Took him a whole day. He hadn't caught anything but leaves and finally lost it in the rocks.

The trap—not Ray's but the real kind, maybe three feet long—was immersed with the open end upstream. Fish came along and, funneled by the narrowness of the stream or by a weir—a fence of stones or sticks—some swam into the cone. Having swum into the pointed end, unable to swim backwards and without room to turn around, they were trapped by the current.

That was the amazing thing: they couldn't back up against the current. And human beings had learned how to exploit that weakness of fish to catch them and eat them.

Willa shivered. This was hand-to-hand combat. Sure, she'd eaten lots of fish in her life, but never had she stolen them from their lair for her direct consumption. She already hungered for their flesh.

She was getting cold sitting still on the stretcher. While the temperature was nothing like the first night, it was still 20 below zero. Only 6:30, but she was exhausted. After the excitement with the search plane and her nap in the snow, she'd spent the day laboring to gather wood and keep the fire going.

She had swum into a trap, eh, couldn't back out, and it was all happening in a swift river of events, swirling and tugging, sucking and ripping, running still. She wanted to sleep.

She spread her parka under the mummy bag, pushed off her outer boots, and slipped into bed. She blew out the alcohol lamp and zipped herself into her cocoon. The frozen tears in the bag hood had mostly evaporated.

The quiet. The time. The space. She was so cut off, so isolated, so tightly wedged into the dark point of the cone. As soon as she blew out the flame at night, low voices and hanging heads filled her mind and the terrible ache burned in her.

Her mind went home. Jean rattled pots in the sink, trying to guess the capital of Mozambique as she listened to "What in the World?" on CBON. Bud watched a broomball match on TV, carving a little canoe from a block of birch. Jordy snored softly with a book on his chest. They all had circles under their eyes.

Willa buried her face in her parka hood and stiffened.

She mustn't think about them. That would just paralyze her. She must think about what she needed to do. Yes, she must find food, figure out how to eat. And do it while she still had food. Do it now.

Work on getting a fire going, keep a fire going, don't let it go out . . .

I'll get more wood, Daddy, the fire needs more wood.

Good idea, Tiger. There's some nice driftwood down by the canoe . . .

8

The Trap

The morning of her fourth day, Willa sat on the stretcher and heated water for tea and the last of her oatmeal.

She looked across the lake, transfixed by the fact that no one had come for her. Not Bud, not Jordy. No Beaver bushplane full of friendly faces. People always got rescued, didn't they?

So it was true. They tried and couldn't find her. Three search planes came within earshot. If she was only thirty miles off her flight path, how would they find her? They would have to make flights parallel to her route every—what, every mile? every half-mile? Sixty flights to cover one side of her path out thirty miles?

She looked out the window at the cloudless deep blue sky.

It was true. It would have been a miracle if they had found her.

Willa hung her head, heaved a ragged sigh, and clasped her hands between her legs. She imagined news reports. *Lost. Abandoned. Starved. Found frozen to death. The body of a young pilot was found today* . . . Maybe her body would never be found. She might collapse while crossing a bog . . .

Only when the water boiled hard enough to jump out of the pot did she snap out of her trance. She turned the flame down, threw herself onto the stretcher, and shook. At length she raised herself up.

Suddenly she lashed out and kicked the side of the cabin. *Boom!* Jarred the pot of water. Hell, she wasn't dead yet; she was still kicking. *Boom*, she kicked again. She moved the pot back, turned the stove off, and poured in the last of her oatmeal.

Died with her snowshoes on. She giggled, thinking of the old saw about cowboys dying with their boots on.

Yeah, that's more like it, that's more like it, Tiger, said Bud, his hand on her shoulder.

Go for it, Woolly! yelled Ray across the rink.

You'll do fine, honey, just jump right in, whispered Jean as Willa gazed at the stage from the wing.

She picked up a couple of sticks left over from her snowshoe-building and began drumming a quick beat on the stretcher frame. Ta-ta-ta-*tum*. Ta-ta-ta-*tum*. *I'm still alive, I'm still alive.* Give it a kick, give it a kick—ka-*boom!* She scrambled to the door, leaped outside, and began drumming on the fuselage. Ba-ba-ba-*boom!* Ba-ba-ba-*boom!*

She announced her message to the cosmos, then bounced back inside and sat in the co-pilot's seat, puffing.

She would keep a fire going and build a fish trap. A step at a time, she would do whatever it took to get her ass home.

After she finished her tea, she went back out, tied on her snowshoes, and built a new fire using mainly green branches.

Once she got a good blaze going, she went into the aspens near the lake and gathered a dozen straight, young, slender sapling trunks about five feet long and no thicker than a broom handle at their base. She brought them back to the fire. Sitting on a cushion of spruce boughs, she trimmed the twigs off the whip-like saplings and whittled the stout ends down to the thickness of a finger.

Working from what would be the tail end, Willa tied the small ends of the long ribs together. She tried tying the ribs on with spiraling rounds of cord, but the ribs collapsed instead of forming an open tube. What was stiffer that she could curl in such a tight circle? If only she had some fiberglass rod or some wire. Wire? The cable. There was a coil of cable in the footwell of the co-pilot's seat. Willa retrieved it. Looked like a spare rudder or aileron cable. A piece of cardboard was taped to it that said R. LANDRY – PEAWANUCK.

Using the pliers from the toolkit, Willa cut the terminals off both ends of the cable and peeled off a strand of wire. The strand was almost twelve feet long. She wound one end around a rib near the closed end. To wind the wire around the next rib, she had to twirl the wire around the long rib. She began a spiral of wire and gradually widened the tube over the next foot of its length to the diameter of a pant leg. She maintained that diameter for another foot and a half before she started flaring the basket out into a funnel shape. As the diameter expanded, the gaps between the ribs became too wide, so she worked in some filler ribs.

The basket trap took shape. The funnel-shaped mouth led into a tube section that tapered off at the end. Around the rim of the mouth she coiled a couple of slender three-foot lengths of aspen and fastened them to each of the rib ends with a twist of wire. The opening was almost a foot and a half across, and the length of the trap was a little over three feet.

It occurred to Willa that if the thing did catch any fish, it would have to be sturdy enough to be lifted out of the water on a line without falling apart. The spiral weft wire, circling the trap from end to end like a corkscrew, would surely give it that strength.

She picked a point behind the bell on the stoutest rib, where the wire crossed, and attached a wire loop. Now she could hook a line to the trap.

It was done. She'd have to find the right place to try it out.

Willa built up the fire again and then packed her small duffel bag for a short expedition. She made a thermos of tea, stowed a couple of goat bars, and packed a skein of cord for the fish trap. Putting her arms through the straps of the duffel bag, she could wear it like a backpack. She tucked the trap under her left arm, took the ax in her right hand, and started off across the low, frozen bog that separated her landing lake from its nearest neighbor to the northeast.

She knew that the lakes in that region were interconnected and flowed to the north and northeast in long chains toward Hudson Bay. What she was looking for was a place where one lake narrowed and drained into another, where the current would be fast and the ice thin. A place above or below the rapids or in the narrows, the sort of place where Bud had showed her and Ray how to fish.

The day turned out mild. As the temperature edged above zero, Willa had to unzip her parka to avoid overheating. She found no direct outlet at the northeast end, but after crossing a nubbly marsh, she found another lake. She stopped and ate one of Jordy's goat bars, then headed across the second lake.

The snow was deep, and even with snowshoes Willa found that traveling was strenuous. It was easiest away from shore on the lakes. There the wind had rolled the snowflakes into tiny balls and packed them solidly into a dense crust. On it her snowshoes sank less than an inch.

Near the end of the second lake, Willa could see the shorelines converging toward a channel feeding into yet another lake. There would be a stronger current in the channel and the ice should be thinner—just the conditions she was looking for. Before reaching the channel, which appeared to be fifteen or twenty feet across, she made her way to the edge of the lake and walked along the shore.

When she was alongside the head of the channel, she stopped and considered her task. She would have to clear the snow away from the ice. But she had no shovel. She would use one of her snowshoes. Rather than hop around on one snowshoed foot, with the other foot plunging through the crust, she took both snowshoes off. She used one snowshoe like a rake, dragging back snow until she had uncovered the ice. She punched it with a stout branch, then carefully tried her weight to see if it would hold up. It held, so she raked away snow a little farther out and tried it again, proceeding this way until she was in the middle of the channel. She was grateful that the snow there was only a foot and a half deep.

At the midpoint she cleared an area large enough to allow for the hole and some space in which to move around it. She then picked up her ax and began chopping into the ice. Each blow exploded sharp chips upward, so she closed her eyes protectively just before the ax bit. Too bad she didn't have an auger like they had at the lake cabin when she was a girl. They had gone up on weekends during the winter to ski and snowshoe, but the cabin didn't have a well, so they drilled a hole in the lake ice for water.

Willa had always helped Bud and Ray shovel the snow away. Then Bud would start the hand auger. Willa tried to turn it, but she didn't weigh enough then to make the blade bite. Ray couldn't make much progress either. When the hole reached through the ice to the water, Bud would hand Willa the slush scoop and she'd dip the slush from the hole, with Bud warning her not to drop the scoop in the lake.

Daddy, I see a fish! Willa remembered peering down into the blue-green water through the silvery tube of ice. They always covered the hole with a board and shoveled snow over it when they left. "That's so the fish don't jump out," Bud had told her.

Willa worried that she might suddenly chop through to the water and lose her grip on the ax, so she stopped to tie cord around her waist and then to the ax handle. She couldn't afford to lose the ax. The ice proved to be half a foot thick, much thinner than it would be in the rest of the lake, where the current was calm. Lake ice commonly froze to a depth of three feet. So far, so good.

Penetrating to the water, Willa saw that it would be tricky enlarging the hole without soaking herself with the backsplash. Instead she cut a circular trench a yard in diameter and deepened it until the plug of ice was free.

The work was arduous and she had to pace herself. She laid her parka aside and worked in her snowsuit, unzipped to the waist. Her thick hair kept her head warm. It was nearing mid-afternoon; the sun was shining and the air was still. She paused to grab a goat bar and her thermos of tea. The snow on the lake was dazzling. Black spruce crowded down to the shores, flanked by thickets of leafless aspen.

At last Willa had the ice plug free, but lifting it out was frustrating. She had no way to get a grip on it without becoming soaked. When she tried to bury the ax blade in it, the ice plug split in two. She must not get wet, she must not get wet . . .

Then inspiration struck. After untying the cord from her waist and the ax, she cut a couple of spruce boughs, jabbed them into the water to wet them, and laid them upon the two pieces. Within fifteen minutes the water had frozen enough to enable her to remove the chunks by pulling on the boughs.

Now she had a hole large enough to push the fish trap through. Slush floated in the black water. She scooped it out with a snowshoe and then knocked the snowshoe on the ice to shake the water off.

With a rush of excitement she picked up the trap. Oh, God, was it really going to work? "Help me, Ray," she said, tying the cord to the loop on the trap. She cut one of the spruce boughs free from its ice chunk. She pushed the mouth of the trap down, then pushed the tail into the water, tucked it under the ice with the stick, and felt the current gently take the trap downstream. She let the cord play through her hands a few yards, cut it, tied the end to the spruce bough that was still attached to its ice chunk, and buried the anchor in the snow.

As a child she hadn't bought Bud's first explanation for

covering the hole in the ice when they were at the cabin. For one thing, Ray was smirking. "C'mon, Daddy, you're joking me," she had told Bud. Of course he was; he admitted it. That was when she first heard about the insulating properties of snow.

Now she gathered an armload of sticks and boughs and laid them over the hole. Then she scooped snow over them, hoping to insulate the hole against freezing overnight. If only she had a snow shovel.

Her trap now hung in the current, waiting for some whitefish or northern pike to happen along in the narrow channel.

She stood and raised her face to the low-hanging sun and watched the white clouds of her breath float up and disappear. She had never before prayed for luck with fishing, but now she stilled her thoughts, opened herself to the silence, and let her simple prayer for food follow her breath into the deepening sky.

Willa put her parka on, tied the snowshoes to her feet, and headed back to her camp. The hike would take close to an hour. She wondered if the trap would really work. Maybe she had forgotten something, something she didn't know about. She would just have to wait and see.

The sun had sunk low; the temperature was falling rapidly. Her steps scuffed rhythmically. She hadn't heard the sound of an airplane for the past twenty-four hours. As Willa made her way across the lake, dread whipped her like a cold wind. She gazed at the trackless immensity surrounding her, all growing blue in the deepening twilight. Emptiness rolled in like the breakers on Hudson Bay.

Her plants. Jean would water them, perhaps even talk to

them. But she probably didn't know about the tapes Willa played for them. Willa felt a twinge of regret for choosing not to go to Meeting with Jean. Sometime after she turned fifteen, she couldn't handle the long silences of Quaker worship anymore. She preferred to go for a walk. Surprisingly, Jean had told her to go ahead and walk, to listen for what "spoke to her condition."

Bud long ago said he belonged to the church of the woods. His pew was a log somewhere. Willa's own place she hadn't found yet.

She reached the middle of the first lake from the plane. Her steps slowed and then she stopped. She squatted down. Silence surrounded her. For a long while she held still in the emptiness. Then she became aware of her breathing and stood up. The moon was rising. She wondered what the name of this lake was.

Maybe it was time she gave up waiting for them. Time she walked out. She resumed shuffling on toward camp. Even in the growing darkness her tracks were easily visible.

Maybe she should just quit with the fire. It was a waste of energy. Just focus on getting out.

It could take days, maybe weeks. She would have to make snow shelters. That would take a shovel of some kind. And a toboggan, so she wouldn't have to carry everything on her back through the deep snow. And food. What if there were no fish in the trap tomorrow? What else could she eat?

Rabbits? She didn't want to kill things. Still, if she were starving she would take a rabbit, if she could. If she needed it and the animal was given, she would apologize and give thanks to it, the way the native people did.

Moose, caribou—how in the world would she take such huge animals? She didn't have a gun and couldn't dig a pit in frozen ground . . . Sometimes you could see beavers and martens, but how would you catch them? Crows—forget it, they were way too smart.

Oh, dearly beloveds, what was she gonna do? She hoped that Ray, since he was dead, would be able to watch out for her, send her some hints . . .

Back in the plane, Willa cooked the Chicken Pilaf dinner. The name was far more colorful than the glop in the pot, but it tasted pretty good. As she ate, she scanned the airplane to see where she could remove a section of the aluminum shell to make a shovel and a toboggan. The wings. Check the wings.

After her meal Willa went down and lifted a wing up to slide the snow off, then dropped it back. It was heavy, but she could lift it.

She scanned it in the night glow of stars and early moonlight reflecting in the snow. It was solid rivets.

A wing had seemed a perfect place from which to remove a flat sheet of aluminum, but not with all those rivets. There was hardly a place to put her hand without covering rivets. Getting a sheet off would take forever. And the piece would be so distorted and full of holes that it would be useless.

She returned to the fuselage and settled on using the section running from the right door back to the tail. Removing such a large piece of the shell would open up a big hole in the plane, of course. Her shelter and her fortress.

Yet if she stayed with the plane and wasn't found, she would have wasted whatever chance she had to make a trek back to civilization. If she could get enough food together to last several days, she'd go for it. The rule about staying with the plane—when you had no radio communication and the wreckage was hidden in the bush, what was the point?

She would make the shovel first. Already she could have used one for the fish trap, and clearing snow for fires. And she wanted to experiment with building a snow shelter. Once she left the plane behind, she would have to make her shelters with whatever nature provided—and there certainly was plenty of snow. Bud's interminable tutorials on survival no longer seemed like just a personal obsession.

The first time she and Ray had gone winter camping with Bud, he had made a snow hut. At age nine, Willa couldn't bring herself to stay in it; it was too small and tight. Even Ray couldn't coax her. She insisted on sleeping in the tent. On a later trip she helped make the shelter.

Bud had bent four aspen saplings into the center and tied them together to form the corners of a shelter.

"Tiger," he had said, "why don't you take the Swede saw and cut these little trees off next to the ground, there, the ones inside the square?" He began weaving branches up the sides.

"Poor baby trees," Willa had said as she struggled mightily with the saw on one of them. It jerked each time she tried to make a stroke.

Bud had looked at her. "Tiger, let me show you something," he said. He took the saw and knelt beside the sapling. "Sometimes the way to do something hard is to do it gently. Start out easy, and see how it makes a slot?"

"Yeah," Willa had answered, paying close attention.

"Well, you want to hold the saw steady, don't let it flop sideways, see, and just work it back and forth gently so it makes a slot for itself until the slot goes through the wood. Don't need to be in a hurry. Okay?"

"Okay!"

"And then kind of watch so the tree doesn't lean back and squeeze the saw blade. Just push it the other way."

"I see, Daddy. Let me, let me."

Bud and Ray had thatched the sides of the shelter with spruce boughs, and then together the three of them had shoveled snow over everything, leaving a smoke hole and an entry hole. Inside they built up three beds of snow along the walls and then scraped the ground clear for a fire in the center.

"Dad?" Willa had said.

"Yeah, Tiger?"

"Won't the fire melt the snow and make it drip all over us?"

Bud had laughed. "That's good thinking, Tiger! Yes, it will melt the snow—but just a little. Any drips will follow the spruce boughs down to the ground. We'll stay toasty and dry."

While they worked, Bud had told her a story about a brave orphaned native girl who rescued her brother after he was kidnapped by raiders. They escaped through the forest in winter, scooping out shelters in snowdrifts along the way. Ray lay rolling his eyes at the idea that a little sister could rescue a big brother.

Willa laughed, realizing now that Bud had probably made up

the story on the spot. She entered the plane and sat down on the stretcher. She was so tired she could hardly push her boots off.

It was dark. The metal work would start tomorrow. She got ready for bed and slipped into her sleeping bag.

Tomorrow she would build a snow shelter, she thought as she tied her bandana and stocking cap over her face and snugged down the mummy hood. Who knew, this might be her last night in the belly of the grasshopper.

She envisioned the trap floating in the current and dreamed of being on a train. On the end of the train were several flatcars carrying helicopters. She wandered through the cars and found everyone waiting for her in the dining car. *Willa!* someone said. *Where have you been? We've been waiting for you.* She tried to explain. They all got off in Montreal, and Willa was alone on the train again. The helicopters were gone.

9

Running Out of Food

On the morning of the fifth day Willa had a Texas Chili dinner for breakfast. She had finished off the oatmeal the day before. As she held her tea in both hands, she brooded on the fact that her food was nearly gone. She'd tried eating less to stretch it out, but she couldn't help herself. Too hungry. Besides, if she was going to starve, what difference did it make if it was a day sooner or a day later?

Enough of that. She gathered her gear and struck out for the fish trap. It was not bitterly cold; her thermometer read 7 degrees above zero. When she arrived, she removed the cap of snow and boughs over the hole and broke a thin rug of ice. The pieces clinked against each other. Hardly breathing, she pulled on the trap.

The current created a little drag as she pulled on the line and the glistening sticks broke through the black water. Nothing. The dripping trap held nothing. Disappointment flooded Willa's mind. What was wrong? Why wasn't it working? She stood and pondered the question, feeling small and alone, wondering what Bud would advise.

She looked about at the still panorama. Spruce was interspersed with aspen, brush, dry cattails, and a few birch. Swales of bog edged the forest, and fingers of unbroken snow ran to the shores of the lake. She dropped the trap into the hole again, eyes blinking back tears of frustration.

Suddenly she saw—it just bobbed there near the surface, clinking among the ice chunks. Of course! It was floating up under the ice! It needed to be weighted down somehow. A rock—impossible to find under all the snow. It would have to be something from the plane, a chunk of metal. She carefully tethered the trap so it wouldn't blow away, covered the hole, and headed back.

On her way, Willa raced through a mental inventory of everything that was in or a part of the plane, but nothing sensible had come to mind by the time she got there. She stood in front of the fuselage. The nose cone on the propeller looked like a helmet. She considered beating it off with the ax, but then she remembered that the landing gear had been clipped by a ledge of rock. She walked toward the shore of the lake, pushed through the brush, and easily found the ledge.

A little prospecting in the snow with a stick turned up a flat rock the size of a shallow cigar box. She hefted it. Good size; it would work. She would put the rock in the nylon bag that had held the freeze-dried dinners and tie it to the retrieval line on the trap.

Although she was hungry, Willa grabbed the nylon bag and returned with the rock to the hole in the ice. She tied the weight to the line about two feet from the trap, so that the trap would drift up in the current not far from the bottom. Just as Bud used to rig their lines to catch walleye. He had attached heavy sinkers to anchor the line to the bottom, and then the bait drifted upward a short way.

Willa lowered the trap and its anchor into the water. The current caught the basket and tugged it downstream as the stone pulled downward. She felt the cord go slack, then pulled it gently taut and anchored it. She stood and looked at the hole, at the white nylon cord running into the curdled black water where glassy shards of ice jostled.

That would have to be it. Now the basket was hanging down where it belonged.

Willa walked back to home base with more spring in her step. Maybe it was crazy, feeling happy when she was nearly out of food, but she believed that somehow the trap would work. She crossed the strip of lakeshore marsh and entered the band of trees that guarded what had been home to her for five days now. Fifty yards from the tree-smacked fuselage, she stopped. "Will you look at that parking job?" she said, shaking her head.

She climbed inside and fixed a meal of curried bean soup. As she chewed the little lumps slowly, she studied the carcass of the plane from the inside. Turning to the left side of the fuselage, she mentally marked the point where the bulkhead walled off the cargo hold from the tail section, so she could locate it on the outside. Cutting a hole there would at least leave her sleeping chamber intact. She tipped up the pot and waited for the last bean to slide into her mouth, set the pot down beside the stove, and stepped out.

She rested the ax on the trampled snow beside the tail of the plane and scanned the smooth, enameled surface of the grasshopper. *Excuse me, Mr. Grasshopper, but I need to take some of your hide.*

With her ax she carefully sliced through the aluminum, starting at the bulkhead and working toward the tail. It was clumsy work at first, until she felt the weight of the metal sheet and found the best angle of attack.

Punk! Brang! The fuselage resounded with each blow. The metal was thinner than she'd imagined. She would probably need to double it over. She made a cut along a row of rivets about the length of her ax handle and then started down on a vertical cut.

Her aim evolving with the work, she removed a section about one ax handle long and half an ax handle wide, which she planned to fold in half. The shovel blade would be about fifteen inches square and double the thickness of the plane's skin.

Once the perimeter of the piece was cut, she set about freeing it from the rivets by prying it up with the ax blade. She jimmied and chiseled and finally got it off. Inside the plane, she folded the stretcher to clear a workspace in the hold and flattened the bubbled sheet of aluminum on the floor with the broad side of the ax head. After folding the sheet in half, she pounded the crease flat. She went down to the aspen grove, cut a three-foot handle from a sapling, brought it back, and laid it upon the shovel blade.

Now, how was this going to work?

She envisioned one possible fix after another, and decided to carve a wedge on one end of the handle, insert it between the folded halves, and hammer the aluminum around it. As she pursued this awkward task, she saw that she would need to fasten the mated edges of the blade together.

With a pair of pliers she folded the edges over and crimped them tight. In her gloves her fingers grew cold gripping the frigid metal, and she stopped now and then to plunge her hands into her hair inside the parka hood.

Something more was needed to secure the handle in its channel. As it was, the handle would pry the folded aluminum apart. This problem stumped Willa for the moment. She could search the aircraft for small nuts and bolts. She could make a series of holes around the channel . . . but what about stitching the sheet metal together by lacing cord through the holes? Ah! The cable wire!

The idea developed quickly. Willa made a series of small holes along both sides of the channel by driving the punch on the multi-tool through with the ax head. She then threaded wire through the holes, tightly wrapping it around the channel, running the wire three times through each hole. The result looked like a prop for a scarecrow, but the handle was secure in the blade.

Willa hefted the little shovel. The blade had dished a bit from the hammering, but it would work. She tossed a few scoops of snow with it and crowed with delight.

He wasn't pretty, but he could type!

Triumph number three—she'd built a pair of snowshoes, she'd made a fish trap, and now she had a shovel.

"I'm going to save my own butt," she said aloud. "God help me, I'm gonna get myself outa here. And I'm going to call this lake 'Lake Goodbye.' "

The only time a boy had asked her out, Lonnie Kingfisher, they'd gone to the Spot and had malts, discovered they'd both read Ruby Slipperjack and Farley Mowat, and forgot all about the movie. His dad was a miner; they moved away during the summer.

Willa knew what most boys thought of her. Too smart, too independent. That was all right with her. She had a life, and she had a few friends—real friends, who didn't care if she wore trendy clothes or hung out with the right people. Nobody else her age had a pilot's license.

She wondered what her young friend Maelyn Jossil was doing. Maelyn had cystic fibrosis, but she treated her sufferings like a form of gravity, necessary to keep her tethered to the ground. And so she was always on her toes. She starred as the Princess Turgid in a film Willa made when she was fifteen. And Bergie—what was he up to? Bergie was one of her lifelong guy friends. Such a comic but somewhat weird.

Well, they were all kind of weird, come to think of it. Like her. Being somewhat weird was why Willa was welding a helmet in shop class. She wanted to name it Irene. Good Knight Irene. Her shop teacher, Mr. Beamish, didn't get the joke or why she and two of her classmates laughed and giggled a lot. He was surprised when they turned out to do good work.

The joke grew stale and the art went out of it, just when Willa felt the wave coming down, about the time she was going through the limp in her monthly pace—the limp where both knees hit the ground.

Willa glanced at her watch—4:00 p.m. She had concentrated so hard on the shovel that the lateness of the hour startled her. The sun was near setting. But she could still dig a snow shelter. She wanted to try her new shovel, as tired and hungry as she was.

Willa found a plump drift near the grove of spruce where the plane was lodged. She visualized a chamber within it. She dug a pit to the ground, some three feet down, where the entrance would be. At the bottom she removed her snowshoes and started burrowing inward. She kept the opening as small and low as it could be, while still leaving room to move in and out of it.

Willa dug into the drift far enough to crouch inside the entrance, rested a minute, then resumed digging. She sliced at the snow with her shovel until the rubble got in the way, and then she removed it. Beyond the vestibule area, the ceiling of the tunnel was too low to sit or kneel; it was barely wide enough to turn around. She would have just enough room to lie with her gear beside her. A small space would be easier to keep warm with her body heat.

The job took a lot of lizardly scooting and squirming. The moon had risen as Willa finished hollowing out her tight quarters. Jamming her slender flashlight into the wall of her new cave, she lay down the crackling tarp that had been folded in the bottom of the survival kit, then the stretcher cushion and her sleeping bag. She retrieved the dimming flashlight, rested on her stomach, and let her breathing settle down.

What a day. Fixing the fish trap. Making a shovel. Digging out the shelter.

Willa wriggled out of the cave and threw herself into building a fire to dry out her icy mitts and cook her evening meal. Nearby lay a pile of dry branches and sticks gathered for last night's fire. She arranged a nest of tinder and twigs in the ashes. She had to nurse the fire along carefully, but fatigue had worn her patience thin and made her clumsy. She dumped a good third of her Mountain

Stew in the snow by accident. She picked out the chunks and ate it anyway. "Get your Mountain Stewcones here!" she sang out.

After eating she stood looking at the twinkling myriad of stars. A light aurora in green and pink played over them. It was like organ music in light.

Would the chords grow bold and daring? It was too cold, and Willa was too tired, to wait to find out. Her breath rose in lazy clouds as she turned away from the embers of her fire. She slithered into the cave, lit a candle, and got ready for bed.

When Willa was at last snugged into her sleeping bag, with the stretcher cushion and the tarp between herself and her bed of snow, she blew the candle out and lay back. Despite her throbbing weariness, she couldn't fall asleep. Maybe it was the novelty of bedding down in a snowdrift; maybe it was the rising moon, or maybe the prospect of running out of food. Not to mention that she was about to cut loose the hope of rescue and strike out on her own.

She stared into the darkness, and there were Jean and Bud and Jordy huddled together. Remorse, fear, and doubt heckled her. Here she was; days had gone by and she had almost no food left. She could die out here, never see her family again. She felt like a sack of sand. Couldn't hold herself up, couldn't breathe. The lining of her skull was aflame, her brain full of smoke. She was trapped in a furnace, a freezer, a vacuum, a vise.

She strained with every cell of her being to communicate to them that she was alive. "I'm coming," she whispered. "Tell them, Ray. I am coming home. I can do it—I *will* do it." She saw Bud sitting on a log with bowed head.

You don't know me, Dad. You're gonna have to stew until I show you. For how could he know she had the stuff? Where had he been for the last six years?

"Go for it, Woolly," said Ray. She looked at Ray. He was— why, he was just fifteen years old. *Ah, Ray, I've passed you. I had to keep going, Ray. But I still need a spy in the sky, brother.*

Jean's eyes were closed. *Yes, Momma, all the world's a stage, and sometimes I have to make up my lines as I go along.*

The snow cave was utterly quiet. Willa gazed into the dark, blood drumming in her temples. "Once I was a caterpillar," she said to herself, remembering a play Jean had written for her and her friends. "Now I'm in my cocoon."

Willa dried her face with the bandana, stretched herself inside the sleeping bag, and thought of the fish trap.

O God, let there be fish waiting for me tomorrow.

She held her breath: what was that? Wolves were singing far off. Their warbles rode for miles across the waves of arctic air to reach her through the doorway of her snowy lair.

Their cries sounded almost human. She remembered the old man in Red Lake, Gordon Savaat, telling her about the wolves. It wasn't in pain or grief that the wolves sang. They sang of where the caribou were, fifty or a hundred miles away. They sang of a kill or the death of a member of the pack.

The wolves probably knew where she was, but they wouldn't bother her. They were shy of humans and the scent of fire.

She saw the wind riffling their fur as they stretched their muzzles to the starry heavens, and sleep at last took Willa to its warm den.

10

Fish

Willa awoke warm and comfortable in the gray light of the snow cave. It was Day Six. Light blazed at the entry hole beyond her feet. She stretched and squirmed inside the bag. Mmm. How stiff she was! Digging out the cave last night. And the temperature—so mild. She dozed a few minutes longer, then unzipped her bag and pulled the thermometer out of her duffel—30 degrees! Sleeping in the cave was far more comfortable than in the plane.

Willa shuffled into her snowsuit and parka, hustled out of the cave, and laid the thermometer on the edge of the pit at the opening. She gathered an armful of sticks and built a fire. Outside, the thermometer read 8 degrees above. In the plane the temperature had stayed nearly the same as outside. She pondered this fact as she made a hot breakfast soup of the last food packet in her pantry, some dried corned beef. Nothing left now but three of Uncle Jordy's goat bars.

Now her life would depend on the fish trap. A tremor shook her. Before long she would be hungry again.

She quickly finished eating, tied on her snowshoes, picked up her ax, her shovel, and the duffel bag, and traipsed off toward the third lake, toward the fish trap. Would there be fish? Willa broke off the anxious thought. Either there was something in the trap or there wasn't. No point in worrying about it in advance.

Her trip to the site took only about fifty minutes this time; she had created a path. She uncovered the hole and cleared out the new ice, then untied the retrieval cord from its anchor and pulled. More drag than before. Of course—the stone hung on the line. The rig itself now weighed more. She pulled it along until the sticks broke the surface. She saw fishtails.

"Eeeeeehaahhh!" she whooped as she pulled the trap out of the dark water and away from the hole. She lifted the basket and slung two long, glistening fish onto the snow, where they writhed sluggishly, red gills gaping, eyes shining like moonstones. She bent over them. Whitefish, three to four pounds apiece. Yes, yes, yes!

She jammed her mitts in the pockets of her parka and pulled out the knife blade on her multi-tool. Tears of gratitude welled in her eyes as she slit bellies and emptied entrails onto the snow. For this she used her bare hands; she didn't want to foul her mitts with fish guts and slime.

The fish would freeze solid by the time she returned to camp. If she wanted to cut them into meal-sized portions, she'd have to do it now. She sliced the fish into pieces that would fit into her cooking pot. They would have to go in her duffel bag, so she packed them in snow to keep the bag clean and the chunks from sticking together. It wasn't worth the trouble and the mess to remove the scales. She'd just peel off the skin when she cooked the pieces.

Willa scrubbed her hands in snow and wiped them vigorously on her thighs. She clamped them, scarlet and stinging, in her armpits for a few moments and then pulled on her mitts. After resetting the trap, she strode back toward camp with her catch.

She couldn't believe it. The trap had worked. It had actually worked! If she could stock up half a dozen fish like these, she could take off. She would have a chance to make it. She was going to make it. Yes!

Once, long ago, she had been fishing with Ray from Jordy's dock on Copper Lake.

Look, Ray, look!

Woolly, you caught a fish! Ray had just hauled five-year-old Willa's rod and reel out of the lake where she'd accidentally cast it and handed it back to her. She then reeled in a small bluegill. *Nice going, Sis!*

Pacing on, Willa licked her chapped lips and whistled like a spring lark gone hoarse—airy tunes set to the rhythm of her quick gait. When she reached camp, she put all the fish portions but one in the plastic bucket and pressed the lid down. Now that she was storing fish in it, she would have to contrive a way to keep the lid secured, other than by forcing it down until the plastic tabs locked. It was hard enough getting off a lid like this when the bucket was at room temperature, but out here the cold plastic was rigid and unyielding.

She melted a potful of water and put in the portion of fish she had kept out of the bucket. After the flesh turned milky white, she poured the broth off into the smaller pot and then turned back to the fish. Carefully she lifted the skin away, separated a forkful of meat from the bones, and placed the steaming mound in her mouth. She closed her eyes as she chewed and savored the succulent flesh.

God, it was good! She took another forkful. It was gone

quickly. She reheated the broth and drank it down.

Sated, she heaved a great sigh. This was food for both body and soul. She had caught it herself, courtesy of aboriginal technology. Come to think of it, she was walking on aboriginal technology, too.

Fed and fired by her success, Willa rose and looked at the fish bucket. She needed a simple way to secure the lid. Cable wire—that would work.

The heavy wire handle on the bucket wouldn't help on the hinge side, but she saw a way to make it form part of the latch on the other. When she tried to bend it with a pair of pliers from the plane's toolkit, however, she failed. The wire was too tough to work with. Instead, she pried the handle out of its holes and punched corresponding holes through the edge of the lid with the multi-tool. On one side she looped a single length of wire three times through the lid and the handle hole to form the hinge. On the other side she twisted several strands of wire together as a unit and wired the lid down. That would be the latch. If an animal tipped the bucket over, the lid would stay on.

Next she turned to the task of wresting a toboggan from the shell of the aircraft. Her watch read 11:00 a.m. The operation was going to ventilate the cabin big time—no turning back after this. But she had the snow cave. She had the shovel. She had snowshoes. And now she had a working fish trap.

It was time to go.

As with the shovel blade, she began by cutting one side of the piece she needed. Once she had cut the borders of the sheet, she pried and pulled it free from the rivets holding it to the frame. She worked slowly and carefully to keep from tearing and distorting the metal.

Around two o'clock in the afternoon she looked up from her work. The fire was dying. She took a deep breath. If she was going to keep a fire going, it would eat up all her time. She would never finish the toboggan. She eyed the bits of twigs and chaff on the snow.

Wait—she could build a sign out on the lake! That would free her from tending the fire, and might even be more visible from the air.

She tied on her snowshoes, picked up the ax, and gathered a bundle of spruce boughs. She dragged them out to the lake and began arranging them in a big arrow pointing to the Cessna. She made five or six more trips to cut as many boughs as she could carry. The sides of the V were twelve to fifteen feet long, the shaft twenty. The job took her two hours, but when it was done, it was done. It didn't need constant attention. Feeling much more at ease, she returned to the toboggan project. Why hadn't she thought of a sign before? One of those planes might have seen it!

The toboggan was bound to be another aboriginal invention, eh? This was too strange. She was taking medical supplies to the aboriginals in the white man's airplane, which crapped out and nearly killed her. And aboriginal "medicine" was saving her skin. Was this the humor of the Great Spirit?

Everything that had worked to keep her alive these six days had been given to her. Now everything made sense. Make-believe with Jean. Camping with Ray and Bud. Building a canoe with Jordy. The welding class.

A sense of gratitude overcame her. She dropped into a crouch upon her snowshoes, held her mind still, and allowed the thoughts to settle like the last snowflakes of a departing storm. "I am alive and I have my wits and I'm going to keep pushing on," Willa whispered to herself.

The light had faded while she was freeing the metal rectangle. She gazed wearily at the pocked and bent sheet on the trampled snow beside the plane. It looked for all the world like a frozen animal hide. She would finish the job in the morning. She built a fire to cook her supper—fish, of course. Her skill had advanced so much that fire-building was no longer the protracted ordeal it had been.

After eating, Willa sat by the fire on the bucket and stared into the coals. Her mind was transported by the burning embers. The cast-off fish skin burned and sent up delicious aromas. A resin-filled knot took the form of a grotesque wolf's head as it blazed and collapsed. She added more wood. A fiery bird wing took shape and slowly crumbled amid sighs and snaps and fits of smoke.

She brushed a spark from her sleeve. The pain inside arose, as it was in the habit of doing after dark, before the ambulance of sleep swept her weary body away. Tears brimmed and the flames took weird, liquid shapes. Jean, Bud. Jordy. The agony. She could die. *First Ray, now me?*

Willa sat before the fire and shrank to her bones, trembling with exhaustion and fear. Completely alone, totally abandoned. How ridiculous to think she could ever hope to get out of this alive. Wisps of vapor rose from between her feet as tears dropped into the snow. "Stupid!" she whispered.

She inhaled some thick smoke and coughed. The scene was filled with dancing lights. She stirred the fire, added some sticks, and stood up. The crackling flames took hold of the fresh fuel and thrust their glow around her.

The fire burned and fell back again. Fatigue and the brutish cold moved Willa at last to pull the fire apart with a stick and scuff stiffly to the cave. At the entry she untied her snowshoes, stuck them upright in the snow, and crawled in.

On her elbows in the darkness, she found the alcohol lamp, pulled a lighter from her pocket and set the wick burning. Each night since the crash she had been sleeping a full twelve hours, but her body still ached for bed when darkness settled in. Mindful of the unusual warmth of the cave, she stripped down to her long underwear before she zipped herself into the mummy bag and blew out the blue flame.

11

The Toboggan

Willa opened her eyes on the morning of her seventh day. She lay snug in her longjohns in the mummy bag, on top of the stretcher cushion with the folded tarp underneath. Insulating snow surrounded her. One cocoon lay inside another.

Willa pulled on her snowsuit, boots, and parka, then crawled out into the trench, made a fire, and put a pot of snow on. Two bags of jasmine tea remained, but she would save them. She would just eat fish this morning. Fish and hot water. Her stomach gurgled. The sun was clearing the horizon, a dark orange ball. The sky was clear; hardly any breeze stirred. Her thermometer read 5 below zero. That was mild, but it still felt brisk after a night in the warmth of the snow cave.

She ate the boiled fish, dropped the bones and skin into the coals, and reheated and drank the cooking water. It was pretty good. Warm water was precious. It took time and fuel to make. Fortified by her hot meal, she tied on her snowshoes, picked up her duffel bag and ax, and headed for the trap.

All right! There were three more fish in the trap, a three-pound pike and two smaller whitefish that Bud would have called "hammer handles." Willa cleaned and cut up the fish, packing them in snow as before. Since finishing her toboggan would take the rest of the day, she put the trap down the hole again.

Back at camp, on the floor of the cargo bay Willa partly unrolled the section of aluminum, painted side down, that she had peeled from the fuselage the day before. She used the ax head to flatten out the creases and the little volcanoes where the rivets had torn through. About two and a half feet wide and a few inches short of six feet long, the sheet had taken to curling up lengthwise. She carried it outside, set the fish bucket and a piece of firewood upon it to hold it flat, and pondered how to form it and prepare it for towing.

Near the front Willa placed her mummy bag, rolled up in the blue tarp. Behind that she set the rolled stretcher cushion, followed by the green survival kit duffel. Inside the green bag went her smaller personal duffel and the rest of the gear—the mess kit, the stove and fuel bottles, the cable wire, the ax, and the rest. In the rear she set the fish bucket. She would bring it along to store the fish and serve as a camp stool. Marauding animals hadn't caused her any trouble yet, but along the edge of the lake she had seen tracks that might be fox. She couldn't afford to have her food cache plundered.

Willa noticed right away how the sheet metal curled over the blue roll of her mummy bag in the tarp. Both ends wanted to curl up. Maybe she could simply fasten tow lines on either side about a foot back from the front edge of the sheet. The curl would form an effective snow fender, just like a classic wooden toboggan.

On their winter camping trips, she and Bud and Ray had towed their toboggans with a pair of aluminum pipes hooked to web belts around their waists. This had made the towing smoother and prevented the toboggans from running up behind them when they were going downhill.

She had no aluminum tubing, so she cut a six-foot length of aspen sapling that had a broad fork at the top, which she could tie around her waist. But how would she hook the pole to the toboggan? Willa squatted down and massaged her scalp with her gloved fingers. She looked at the flexible metal sheet, then at the pole; she closed her eyes again. She grimaced and went through this routine for a couple of minutes.

Finally she rose, took her ax down to the aspen saplings again, and returned with three sturdy sticks, each about three feet long. She wired them into a stout triangle, then drew the toboggan partway through it. She wired one leg of the triangle across the sheet about a foot back from the front end. Now she could attach her tow rod to the forward point of the triangle, which would act as a yoke. The twelve-inch excess of sheet metal in front would curl over the tarp and mummy-bag roll, and the rest was cargo space.

Willa piled her gear on the toboggan, fastened the tow rod to the front of the triangle with cord, and then tied the fork of the tow rod to her waist. "Hey, everybody, I got hitched!" she announced, dipping a mitt down and tossing a bouquet of snow into the air. She stepped forward, turning to see how the rig was riding. As she pulled the toboggan around and started toward the lake, she saw that things tended to shift around on the metal sheet. The toboggan needed some side rails so that the load could be lashed in place.

It took another hour and a half to cut a pair of slender saplings and wire them to the edges of the sheet. Three crossbars kept the bottom rigid when she drew the lashing tight.

Willa towed the loaded toboggan out onto the lake and walked south for several minutes, then stopped and looked back at the crash site and down at the toboggan. A big red "1," part of the plane's identification number, showed against the white background where the painted side of the sheet curled up in front. "All right!" she crowed, pumping her mitt in the air. "Tomorrow I'm out of here, eh!"

The sun had sunk near the horizon in the southwest, but Willa had one more small project. She returned to the plane and cut another sheet of metal from the fuselage, about fifteen inches square. She flattened it carefully and took pains to manicure its edges with the file on the multi-tool so she and her clothes wouldn't get cut. She could use the square as a snow knife to cut blocks of snow for an igloo, or as a wind screen for the stove. Or a cookie sheet. Every snow queen should have one.

As darkness settled, hunger took command. Willa moved over to the torch tree, built a fire in the pit, and put a frozen hunk of fish in a pot half full of ice. Once the ice melted, she watched to make sure the fish thawed before the water got too hot. One thing she hated was overcooked fish. If she tried to cook a frozen chunk too fast, the outer portion would get tough while the inside was still raw. A good job took time.

While she waited, loneliness and fear weighed in. Tears came, as they did every night. Was she kidding herself? There probably wasn't another human being within a hundred miles. Defeat was inevitable, stalking her like a hungry polar bear. She was lost and helpless.

She pressed the bandana to her eyes.

"Stop!" she cried aloud. "Look what you've done! You've made snowshoes, and a shovel, and a toboggan. You've built a flippin' fish trap, and you're eating the flippin' fish!"

She laughed. She was doing all right, eh. Just tired. She yawned.

God, she had been lucky. If it hadn't been for all the trips with Bud and Ray, she'd probably be dead by now. Bud had been so strict. He had made her and Ray lay out all their stuff and check and recheck their lists. And Jean too, she was stubborn. Not *stubborn* so much; she just knew what she wanted and kept going after it through thick and thin. Ray, he had been good to her most of the time, except when he had wanted to be left alone with his friends.

I'm gonna walk out of here.

She retied the bindings of her snowshoes, trudged out onto the lake, and looked up at the heavens. The moon hadn't risen yet; the chorus of stars was deafening. Each constellation stood out in its full panoply of blazing points—the Big Dipper, Orion, the Navigator's Triangle, Cassiopeia.

Willa had once told Woogy, her literature teacher, about Jordy's lessons on the constellations, and Woogy had loaned her a book of Greek myths. There was one about Cassiopeia, who offended Poseidon, god of the sea, and for that he chained her daughter Andromeda to a rock, where she was at the mercy of a sea monster. Perseus rescued her. Major hero.

Those Greeks were such male chauvinists, Willa mused. They assumed the girl would be helpless. Of course, they did have the legends of the Amazons.

Okay, so she wasn't an Amazon, but she wasn't a helpless waif, either.

Willa walked back to the fire and pushed the pot farther into the coals, squatting so she could feel the heat on her face.

She could do this—she could face the monster alone. Ray— yeah, she had taken up his torch, tried to hold up his corner of the tent, took on his boy bravado. Now she was two years older than Ray was when he died. She couldn't guide her life by his lights anymore. She loved him, but he was on the other side now. And she was still here.

She had to find her own way, by herself—and yet she was not alone, really. This winter wilderness, spattered with thousands of lakes and bristling with black spruce, was vast, cold, and powerful, but it was not evil. And it wasn't a mere whirlpool of brute forces, either. Something delicate, spiritual, brooded out here.

After a while Willa raised her eyes to the spruce boughs above. The branches seemed to form circles in the firelight. They seemed to be reaching around to embrace her. This tree, which she'd tried to burn, still offered her shelter.

She stood up and put more wood on the fire. She unzipped her parka and snowsuit partway and pulled her harmonica out of her shirt pocket, where it had stayed warm. Rocking before the flames, she picked out an old camp tune, "Kookaburra." She had trouble making her lips purse around the holes at first, but it got better as she went.

Supper was ready. She tucked the harmonica away and pulled the pot from the fire. The fish was getting tiresome, but this time she'd used some of the seasonings from the survival pack—salt, pepper, sage. Jordy was a good cook; it was no surprise the food kit held so many seasonings—garlic powder, spices. He was an interesting guy, her uncle.

While she ate in the glow of the fire, she scooped some snow into the fish pot and set it back in the embers. When it came to a boil, she poured the broth from the pot into her mug and sipped the hot liquid. She melted snow in the large kettle and threw her bandana in. When the water boiled, she fished the bandana out with a stick, let it cool a little, and wrung the steaming rag out. It had gotten stiff with tears and snot. Maybe it would dry in the cave overnight.

Before the fire died out, she melted more snow water for breakfast in the cooking pot and dropped in a chunk of fish. She folded the handle and set the pot in the bucket to freeze, pulled the fire apart, and went to the latrine she had established in a windbreak of small spruces. After scrubbing her hands briskly in the snow, she headed for the cave.

Willa was tired to the core. But she felt ready, even eager, to leave the plane and head to the south. That had to be the way to go. Traveling upstream along the rivers and lakes would be easier than cutting across uneven terrain covered with trees and brush. That tack would take her in a south-southwesterly direction, toward branches of the winter roads that led to native communities she'd flown over. She had a plan. It made sense.

If a storm blew in, she would just have to hole up somewhere—dig a snow cave, build a lean-to, or crawl into a pit under a spruce tree. She planted her snowshoes upright, slithered into the snow cave. She stripped down to her longjohns and slid into the mummy bag, laying the ice-starched bandana over her duffel bag.

Tomorrow—if she had enough fish—she would head out. Eventually she would have to come upon people.

12

The Journey Begins

The next morning Willa emerged from her snow cave to find thick, big-flake snow falling and the temperature at 12 degrees above zero. A heat wave! She could smell the ashes of the dead campfire and the scent of the spruces. It was Day Eight.

Willa sucked in a deep breath. As she looked up at the sky, search planes seemed a distant memory. She boiled her breakfast under the tree, ate, and filled her thermos with the hot cooking water. If the trap held any more fish, she would leave. If not, she would wait.

Since her fish-trapping site was to the north-northeast, she wouldn't lose any ground by returning to the plane to launch her journey after she checked the trap. She'd take only her ax and her duffel bag with her now.

As she came within sight of the mounded snow around the hole in the ice where the fish trap hung down, her hope of finding more fish was salted with the knowledge that they would send her on her way. And there they were—two slender pike that reached from her snowshoes to mid-thigh when she held them up by the gills. It was enough.

Willa cleaned and sectioned the fish, breaded the pieces with snow, and stowed them in her duffel. When she got back to the plane, she added the new catch to her larder. The bucket now held fourteen chunks, most weighing around three-quarters of a pound. She would travel for several days and then set the trap in a stream again before she ran out.

Willa rolled the mummy bag up in the blue tarp, tied a piece of cord around it, and set the roll crosswise in the front of the toboggan. She set the fish bucket in next, then the stretcher cushion, followed by the large green survival kit duffel with everything else inside. She tied the shovel and the trap to the toboggan atop the load, fastened the tow rod to her waist, and with no further ceremony headed toward the south-southwest across Lake Goodbye.

The snow fell thickly, without hurry. After about five minutes Willa pulled the toboggan halfway around and turned to look at the place she had called home for seven days. The dismembered fuselage lay worn out, having given its all. One spruce tree stood dark green among its snow-cloaked neighbors; Willa recognized it as the intended torch tree. She bid the tree and the grasshopper farewell. "Goodbye," she said. "I'm out of here."

Snowflakes the size of babies' hands swirled down, and Willa's thermometer read 15 above—amazing. She put it back in its tube, tucked it into a breast pocket of her snowsuit, and left her parka unzipped to vent excess heat. Her snowshoes squeaked and rushed, squeaked and rushed; her pant legs swished and the toboggan hissed, giving a *crunk* whenever it struck a bump. The Raedl Express was on its way.

Within twenty minutes Willa had reached the south end of Lake Goodbye and started across a frozen bog staked with blackened tree trunks. Walking was hard here; her snowshoes sank a foot in the dry, airy snow. She pulled her compass out of a parka pocket. She hadn't needed it in the neighborhood of the plane and the fish trap, but heading off across country would be different. The snow blurred the horizon, and she didn't want to travel in circles.

The going was slow. She wouldn't set any speed records. She had to lift her feet high with each step. Her boots were heavy, her snowshoes were heavy, and a certain amount of snow tended to ride on top of them, adding more weight. After a couple of hours the tendons at the back of her knees ached. Every fifteen or twenty minutes she stopped to rest.

When she halted, the whispering, wild beauty and the sheer vastness of the winter-bound country filled her with awe. When she moved on, the pain in her tendons returned. "Bet my feet wouldn't sink a foot in the Sahara," she muttered, looking out across the white dunes. Of course, she couldn't melt sand and drink it, either.

The patterns sculpted by the wind in the snow changed constantly. Successive snows had left overlapping layers. One looked like a rippled river bottom, another like plates of white shale shingled over one another. Some areas resembled shallow sawtooth mountain ranges and others the folds of a vast drapery. The shadows were mostly blue, except when snow scattered light at the right angle to make a faint green or red.

After crossing a flat, sparsely wooded plain, Willa entered upon a lake not much bigger than the one she'd landed the grass-hopper on. Eighteen inches of snow lay on the ice, but her snowshoes sank only an inch into the windswept crust. Her squeaking steps sounded a hollow cadence.

By the time she reached the opposite shore, the snow had stopped and the wind was picking up. She was hungry, but she hadn't saved any cooked fish to eat on the way. She would have to eat one of Jordy's goat bars—she had only three left—or build a fire and cook. She pulled her thermos out of her parka and took a drink. Not much water remained and it was getting colder, but it wouldn't hurt the thermos if that little bit froze. The plug made a hollow clunk as she twisted it back in. She ate a bar and resolved to travel a couple of hours more before making camp.

The dull glow of the clouded sun shifted toward the west. Willa stopped and looked around. Her legs ached. She estimated that she had covered as much as eight or ten miles that day, after retrieving the fish trap. Tomorrow she would travel again as soon as she had eaten and melted water for the day. Cover ground; she had to cover ground now.

She saw a thicket of spruce trees up ahead and went toward them to look for shelter for the night. She had already picked up a few dry branches from fallen trees and some loose shreds of birch bark in the last mile or so, expecting to build a fire soon. She was hungry, thirsty, and ready to rest.

As Willa snowshoed up to the spruces, she found that a fallen tree had created a shelter where she could bed down for the night. She carefully opened an entryway into the natural cave of snow-capped branches and arranged her sleeping quarters. Then she gathered more firewood, shoveled out a pit nearby, and soon had a crackling blaze. The warmth bathed her face as she watched the flames.

The fire was friendly. It was alive and kept her company. She missed the grasshopper, yet it was still with her in the toboggan, the shovel, her snowshoe bindings . . .

She removed the lid of the fish bucket to select her supper. "Hmm, let's see, shall I have fish tonight? Or fish? Ah, no. I think I'll have fish instead!" She rolled over in the snow, cackling madly. She lay still for a minute, curled up on her side, then rolled to her knees and rubbed her face with her mitts. *Get a grip, girl.*

She had spent an entire day putting hard distance between herself and the crash site. She was committed now, but as anxious as if she had set out to cross the ocean in a canoe.

Willa dislodged a block of fish from the bucket, put it in the pot, replaced the lid, and sat down on the bucket. She stared into the snapping orange flames as the light of day stole away and the world once again shrank to the limits of her campfire light. A small drop of melted snow fell from above, and Willa's mind floated away.

Ray, please let me go with you. I promise I won't get in the way. I'll . . .

No, Woolly, you can't. I'm going out with the guys and you can't come. We're going out to check traplines. It's too dangerous for a little kid.

Little kid—little kid! You said we were buddies. We ride on the Ski-Doo together all the time. Kirk's brother is only twelve, and he lets him come along.

Woolly, you don't understand. Look, I'll give you something—how about this? My cedar dragon!

I don't want your old cedar dragon, Raybees. You're a mean, sick old dog, Raybees!

Adding more sticks to the fire, Willa sighed deeply and blinked back tears. Ray had walked out, swearing under his breath. That was the night—the night . . . They'd gotten some beer somehow; there weren't any traplines, they went tearing around on the snowmobiles . . .

I am all right, she said now to her family, eyes tightly closed, hands pressing against her forehead. *You know me.*

They must know that she could survive if she had landed safely. She had the stuff. Bud would know. She could not allow her guilt and their fear and grief to keep wearing her down.

Ach—the fish was cooking without any flavorings or spices. She rummaged around in her duffel and found the spice bag. The Tex-Mex spice smelled good. She added a pinch of salt and some garlic powder as well.

When the fish was cooked, Willa ate. She noticed some tiny fat globules floating in the water—they didn't amount to much. She was getting plenty of protein, and maybe a little carbohydrate. More carbohydrate would be good to keep her energy up, but she wasn't sure just where to find it.

Her mind cast about over the frozen land. Cattail roots were said to contain edible starches. And where would she find more fat? From rabbit meat? She had never been interested in hunting game of any kind, other than fish when she camped with Bud. But now her survival was at stake, and her mind pursued the rabbit's flesh without guilt.

She thought about making a snare with fishline from the

survival pack, bending down a sapling and setting it so that it could be triggered to snap up and snare the animal. Somewhere she'd heard of something like that.

Willa melted more snow and filled her thermos, then melted another pot of snow and put a piece of fish in it for breakfast. She let the fish cook slightly and took the pot off the fire. She sat by the fire for a time, thinking about the snare.

The only other mammal she might come across would be a fox, and she'd never heard of people eating fox. Besides, foxes were known for their cleverness, weren't they? They would probably be next to impossible to catch.

Possibly there might be moose around, but she had no means to bring down an animal as large and dangerous as a moose. Deer would never let her get near. She guessed that the other animals that inhabited the region would be hibernating—black bears, otters, squirrels. Female polar bears were hibernating while the males hunted on the sea ice. Neither was likely to wander this far from Hudson Bay in any case. There might be beavers, but they'd be difficult to catch, and they lived in streams where the ice could be thin. Anyway, they were very intelligent, family-oriented animals—the Indian name for them meant "little men." It seemed wrong to kill one.

Weariness hung on Willa, and she began to shiver as the fire died down. She waved her bandana over the coals to drive out the frost from her breath and checked to make sure the lid on the fish bucket was secure.

She crawled under the snow-clad branches that arched over her sleeping bag, sat down, and removed her boots. She pulled the felt liners out and put them back on her feet. She tied the stocking cap and bandana around her face and slipped into the bag, bringing her thermos bottle and the camp stove in with her. She snugged the drawstring of the mummy-bag hood around her face and lay on her side, watching the embers of her fire.

Still alive.

Willa awoke in the night to a strange sound. She raised herself up slightly and strained to see. As soon as she moved, a shadowy form near the fish bucket skittered away. She stared toward the bucket. A fox had probably taken an interest in it. She sank back into her dreams.

13

The Blue Dome

Willa woke as daylight was seeping into the sky. She dressed, legs stiff and sore, trudged around to gather wood, and built a fire for breakfast. The fox had left teeth marks on the bucket and had pushed around the pot with the breakfast fish frozen in the ice. The lid had frozen on the pot, so the fox hadn't touched her fish. The bones and boiled-out fish skin she'd cast aside had been scattered. She took note of the tracks. Sliding the pot into the coals, she cooked the fish, ate, melted some more snow to top up her thermos, and packed her gear for another day's journey.

The temperature that morning, her ninth day, hovered at zero, and the wind was mild. Willa walked steadily, rhythmically, pulling the toboggan along behind her, stopping every half-hour or so for a few minutes to rest. The sky cleared, and the sun, always more or less in front of her unless it was early or late in the day, glared on the snow. She was relieved when she walked through wooded areas, where the glare was less. But the snow was always deeper and softer there, slower going, so she had to stay out in the open whenever she could. Willa grew tired of shielding her eyes with her mitts.

What she needed was a pair of goggles. She remembered seeing pictures—aboriginal people in snowy regions made them by cutting narrow eye slits in a birch-bark or leather mask. She had no pieces of birch bark large enough in her tinder stash, but soon she came upon some birch trees on a riverbank and removed a patch of the stiff, papery bark from one of them. "Naughty, naughty," she scolded herself. It was a camper's sin to remove the bark from a living birch, but she didn't see any downed ones.

Willa pulled her snow-queen cookie sheet from the toboggan to use as a work surface. Squatting with the edges of her snow-shoes over the sides of the sheet, she used the multi-tool blade to cut a mask with wings that she could tuck into her hood over her ears, and she cut narrow horizontal slits for her eyes. She tried the mask on. The slits were a little high, but she remedied that fault by cutting more away at the bridge of the nose.

She looked around. The goggles reduced her peripheral vision, but they were a great relief. The essence of simplicity. Too bad she hadn't kept the lenses from her aviator glasses—she might have been able to fix them in a birch-bark frame. But the mask was very effective at cutting the glare, and her breath wouldn't fog up the slits.

Willa tied her shovel back down along with the fish trap and started off again. Before long she stopped and used her knife to fray the edges of her snow goggles where they rested on the bridge of her nose and on her ears. While she was at it, she ran the slits farther out to the sides to improve the peripheral vision.

For hours she trudged slowly along the trail of frozen water, now traversing a long, narrow lake, now following the shore along a river when the ice was too chancy, now detouring around a stretch of muskeg studded with waist-high tussocks. When her course was set for a few hundred yards more, her mind would turn to pizza, or chem lab, or Lonnie, until she came to a bottle-neck at the end of a lake, sized it up, and took to the shore or tested the ice and moved on.

From time to time a song would rise that matched her steady, shambling gait. She sang "A Song of Peace," a Quaker hymn set to the tune of *Finlandia*, and the spirituals "Swing Low, Sweet Chariot" and "Lean on Me," and she chanted phrases that rose by themselves from the rhythm of her pace. She nibbled at the frozen fish she carried in a plastic bag and sipped water when she paused to rest. At midday, she laid out the tarp and her mummy bag in a sunny windbreak, put her parka back on, and lay down for a cat nap.

In half an hour, becoming chilled, Willa rose, packed up her tarp and bag, and set out again, soon reaching the long, flat expanse of another lake in a chain that stretched on and on. She checked her compass. Still heading south-southwest.

The region Willa was in, the Hudson Bay lowlands, was filled with bogs and streams and crowded with countless long, narrow lakes. As she traveled, she encountered birch and aspen groves amid the black spruce and tamarack. In boggy stretches sometimes light wisps of vapor rose from the ground. She skirted these areas when possible, and crossed them with caution when not. Decaying vegetable matter in the bogs generated heat. Snow often concealed treacherous pits that could soak a leg to the knee or turn an ankle.

Approaching the southern shore of yet another lake, Willa studied a thick field of cattails before her. The snow in the area had a curdled appearance, a sign of boggy conditions. She detached her toboggan, took her shovel and ax, and trod cautiously into the cattails.

The snow was crusty and uneven; there were scattered crevices partially filled with snow. Some of the cattails still had ragged heads, and from these she stripped the silky fluff and filled her pockets. It might be useful for starting fires.

She dug down through the snow and with the ax pierced into the semi-frozen mud. She pulled up some of the cattails and was disappointed to find no plump tubers, nothing but stringy black roots. She caught a whiff of decaying plant matter.

She tossed the dry plants down and heaved a weary sigh. Night was nearing and it was time to find a place to camp. She headed for a haven of spruce trees.

On the southeast side of the grove Willa found a snowdrift a good five feet deep. She dug a trench down to the ground and then excavated a tunnel into the end of the drift. She carved out an entrance and began working her way in. Soon she was backing out to remove loose snow. Occasionally she stopped to rest. Pacing herself was becoming a matter of habit.

The temperature was 6 degrees above zero and dropping; the wind was light. She shed her parka and worked in her snowsuit. She wore the hood up to keep her head dry as she crawled in and out of the growing cavity.

Inside, she carefully shaped a dome overhead and widened the space out enough to place her gear alongside her. She smoothed the ceiling of the dome with her mitts to minimize the loose snow that would drop down if she accidentally brushed against it. She chuckled when she uncovered a twelve-inch spruce seedling beside the spot where her head would lie. "Oh, welcome, little one," she cooed.

The sun had set by the time she finished her work. It was five o'clock. The late western sky was splashed with vivid oranges and salmons behind broken cirrus clouds.

In the light that lingered Willa gathered dead branches from the spruces, snapping off the brittle limbs by hand or with a blow of the ax. Soon a three-quarter moon took over for the departed sunlight, illuminating the snowscape with eerie brilliance. Near the moon was a star so bright that it had to be a planet. Venus? Jupiter?

Willa put her parka back on. She started a fire in the trench outside the snow cave and put a pot of snow in to melt. When she had enough water, she drank and added more snow. Then she put a slab of fish in the pot and added the last of her salt and some sage. She would save the fish intestines next time. They might have valuable fat and vitamins, and might add a different flavor. In another couple of days she would have to fish again.

She finished her meal and leaned toward the fire, her elbows on her knees. On her face she felt the flickering radiance. The smoke was pungent with spruce resin. She unzipped her parka and held her damp mitts toward the flames. Nourishment crept into her body, although she didn't feel full. Soon alertness returned and she stood up. *Ooh!* she groaned as she stretched, wincing at her aching legs. She was tired from the day's travel, but she was not ready to sleep. It was only a little after seven o'clock, and dawn would not come until eight in the morning.

Willa tied on her snowshoes and walked away from the trench

to look around. In the moonlight the world about her was a spectacle of otherworldly beauty. The black spruces were doubly black against the great, endless mantle of glowing snow.

This terrain stretched in all directions as far as she could see. Willa felt as if she were on another planet—or the moon, but no wolves ever howled on the moon. No worms ever digested moon soil. Willa giggled at the idea. A smile remained with her, stretching her fuzzy, chapped lips. She was still breathing, still looking about, still walking out, on the night of her ninth day.

She savored the thought of wolf kinship in that forbidding land. Those wolf folks got to go snuggle up with the family in their dens. Most of them, anyway; there were times, she knew, when individual wolves ran alone. She could relate. Bud had talked at length to her and Ray about wolves on their trips. He'd introduced them to Gordon Savaat in Red Lake, who was full of stories. Gordon had known wolves all his life. They were wild animals, of course, and mysterious for that, but like beavers they shared some traits with humans. Willa liked thinking about it.

It was time to look for more dry branches among the trees. She gathered an armload, then returned to the trench in front of the snow cave. As she sat down on the bucket and built up her fire, she fixed her mind on the task of designing a snare.

She would tie down a sapling so that when an animal tripped it, it would spring up and catch the animal in a noose. It was easy enough to imagine a noose tied to the sapling. But how would it be triggered? The first thing that came to mind was a bow. Tie the thing down with a bow instead of a knot, and let the animal pull the bow. If she fixed the bait to the end of the cord, an animal pulling on the bait would pull the bow. The noose would have to be separate. She'd lay it around the spot where the animal would rise up to grab the bait.

And what about bait? What would entice a rabbit? What did rabbits eat in the winter? Buds of some sort, probably. Willa wondered how long it would take to snare a rabbit using buds as bait, when there were buds everywhere. Maybe if she simply found a trail and hung the snares over it . . . The fox that had tried to get at her fish—maybe she could snare a fox with a piece of fish. She had seen a video about the Yukon one time. People living in the bush trapped martens for their fur. Martens ate fish.

But she was sleepy and cold. She rose and stretched.

After Willa crawled into the cave, she pulled the bucket into the opening and carefully stuffed her duffel bag around it to block the hole. With her flashlight, she found a candle and lit it. Then she removed her parka and boots and slipped into the bag, avoiding contact with the walls. The little cavern of snow was very snug and quiet. The walls glittered in the candlelight.

Willa dwelled for a few moments on the primitive security of her den, blew out the candle, and zipped herself up. She stretched out on her back in the mummy bag on the floor of the silent vault and found that the contour of the ground was like a gentle recliner. It was the most comfortable bed she'd had so far.

Willa lay back and let her taut muscles relax. Her body hummed like a mass of rubber bands letting go of each other. She lay with eyes closed, gradually feeling her body float free in the warmth of her sleeping bag.

Just as she was about to drop into sleep, Willa's eyes flickered open and she noticed a blue haze above her. Had her eyes been affected by the glare of the sun during the day? She pulled her arm out of the bag, held it over her head, and was startled to see the silhouette of her hand! Phosphorescent snow? No. The moonlight was shining through the roof of the cave!

Willa lay back, gazing up at a dome of faint blue light. There was a foot and a half of snow above her, and the moon was shining through it! It was as if she'd hollowed out an azure jewel. She marveled at the physics of snow, how moldable it was, how able to hold in warmth, seal out wind, pass light through.

She lay in a state of wonder, like a small child wrapped in a blue night-cloud.

Vision slipped into dream and she slept.

14

The Storm

Willa stood on the snow at the edge of the grove and tied the fork of the tow rod to her waist. The cave had been so comfortable that she regretted leaving it. It was not even dawn yet. The moon shone like an egg on the western horizon. She had awakened well rested, built a fire and eaten and melted water. This morning of her tenth day, the temperature hung near 12 below, but the air was dead still. It looked like a good day to travel, as long as the wind didn't rise. She trudged away, her snowshoes scuff-crunching in the snow, the toboggan dogging behind her. The red bandana held her stocking cap in place over her face as her breath steamed in the moonlight.

The dream was still fresh. Lonnie had come last night. He had nudged Willa awake; she had touched his face.

Lonnie?

Willa, I know you're on your way. It's hard. Hard to remember, hard to believe, but I know you are. You know, too.

Lonnie, have you been writing poetry again? I'm so hungry. Let's go to Socrates'. I want stuffed grape leaves. And spanakopita.

Willa, Socrates' is halfway to Dryden from Sioux Lookout.

Please, Lonnie?

Okay. We've got to hurry, then.

Yeah.

"Yeah." Willa breathed a puff of steam as she walked in the blue dream world before dawn.

She felt as though she had actually talked to Lonnie. He knew. Her task was simple. Keep moving, stay alive.

She angled toward the south-southwest now as she walked upstream on the long chain of lakes, avoiding dense patches of brush and trees and heavily nubbled bogs. She moved rhythmically on as the stars faded and the sky grew light. In the bitter cold her bandana became encrusted with frost. She was a bearded lady.

After a couple of hours daylight had crept back into the world. The sky was overcast. She would travel all this day, and the day after she would look for a place where she could fish and set snares, and she would build a shelter to last several days. By noon the overcast had thinned; the sun shone wanly and the temperature rose to zero.

In the early afternoon Willa walked up to another cattail bog and stopped to look again for edible roots. She cleared the snow away from a small patch and chopped through the ice below. This time steam rose and she could see dark liquid. Not wanting to plunge a bare arm into the frigid water, she pulled the bread bag out of her duffel and slipped it over her mitt and sleeve. Lying in the snow, she felt in the soft mud for roots. She grasped a gnarled mass, dragged the whole plant out, and slapped the root end down on the snow to clean off the mud.

This time there was something substantial—a brownish twisted root mass. She reached in again and pulled up three more clumps of roots with plants attached. Grasping the stems near the bottom, she scrubbed the roots in the snow to clean off the mud and cleaned the bread bag, too. These tubers had possibilities, although she didn't know just how to cook them.

Willa stood for a moment thinking about the biological activity of the bog. Decaying plant matter generated enough heat to soften the snow on warmer days, and then it would refreeze into a crusty texture. How strange to think that under the snow and ice there was mud and water. What other edibles might lurk down there?

Willa examined the brown, rope-like roots of the cattails. Now that they had been extracted from the bog, they would freeze hard. She opened her knife blade and cut the roots up into the bread bag as if she were preparing a stir-fry.

As Willa walked around the cattail bog, pulling the toboggan in her left hand, she stopped to strip some more fluff from a crop of ragged heads. Suddenly she stepped on the edge of a hole with her left snowshoe and fell sideways. The snowshoe had nearly snapped. She must be more watchful. A twisted ankle could be deadly, and she certainly didn't want to spend a day making another snowshoe. She stuffed the fluff into the nylon bag that had held the meal packets, noticing the tiny seeds on the cottony filaments.

The next lake Willa walked upon ran for miles, like a wide river. Along the way she passed a couple of small, oblong islands. The wind was light, but still it spawned the occasional whirling snow dervish that appeared like a wraith, spun for a minute, and flew apart into iridescent dust. An hour and a half later, the lake narrowed to the mouth of a frozen stream, and she took to the bank until she could safely enter the next lake. It too stretched far into the distance before her. As she stood there in the breeze, her fatigue caught up with her. It was only three o'clock, but she was ready to stop and make camp. She had started very early that morning. Besides, something seemed to be building up in the northwest.

Willa angled back toward shore and aimed for a stand of spruce. Circling around to the lee side, she chose a dune about fifty yards from the trees. She unhitched the toboggan and dug a trench to the ground. The snow was only a couple of feet deep, not deep enough to dig the sort of cave she'd had the night before. But as she shoveled out the trench, she noticed that the snow lifted up in large, light chunks. Maybe she could build an igloo.

Using her cookie sheet and the shovel, she cut blocks the size of file boxes, removed them from the floor area, and stacked them along both sides. She dug a three-by-four-foot vestibule area near where the entry would be. Here she could sit and keep her gear. She extended the trench another six feet beyond it, leaving a foot of packed snow to form a raised sleeping shelf.

Taking blocks from the area around the trench, Willa built up parallel walls roughly ten feet long on each side, overhanging the second row to make the walls tilt inward. Then she stopped to rest. She'd cut and placed thirty-two blocks already. The blocks weren't that heavy, but cutting and stacking them was no picnic. She was too far along to abandon the project now. She sat cross-wise in the vestibule to test its size, her back to one side and her feet pressed against the other.

Willa got up, cut more blocks and stacked them in a third row on each side, and then blocked up the ends. She cut a few armloads of branches from the nearby spruces, bridged the two sides with them, and laid upon them a double row of shallower snow blocks that touched and made a roof. She chinked the cracks with snow wedges and then shoveled loose snow over the structure. Finally, she carved an entry hole into the vestibule.

The work had taken her past sunset, and as the blue light of dusk filled the entry hole, she smoothed the inside walls with her mitts and scraped out the loose snow that had fallen on the floor. She was glad there was headroom to kneel or sit in the vestibule. Crawling back outside, she stacked a few snow blocks near the entry to shield her campfire from the wind. What a lot of work, compared to hollowing out a drift! She would build no more castles like this one.

Willa ached with hunger. She built a fire and put on her pot of fish frozen in water. At long last, after eating the hot, unseasoned fish, she cooked the sliced cattail roots. When they had boiled for several minutes, she began chewing them, a few pieces at a time, swallowing the juice and spitting out the fibrous pulp. The roots were bland but a welcome change from fish, and there did seem to be some starch in them. She ate quickly, for she was cold and tired and wanted to move inside the igloo.

The wind gusted and Willa shivered. Fine snow filled the air and set up a sparkling halo over the fire. She packed snow in the pot to melt for breakfast and went out to gather a little more wood. She could hardly see under the trees. The moon hadn't climbed very high. As Willa dropped her first armload of branches and turned, a blast of wind shoved her back a step. The world was losing its form in blowing snow.

It was time to hang it up. She grabbed the pot from the dying fire and scuttled inside. She blocked up the entry with the fish bucket and the green duffel, lit her alcohol lamp, and laid out her tarp, cushion, and sleeping bag on the narrow sleeping shelf. No sound of the wind outside penetrated the shelter as she rustled about in her tight quarters. The lamp cast a steady, faint glow. She was exhausted, but a feeling of well-being floated up like a sweet scent. Her meal was reaching home. Perhaps the cattails, the carbohydrate. She had eaten only half the roots; she would gather more tomorrow.

Willa sat cross-legged in the tiny vestibule, head in her hands, and pondered her plan for the next day. She had barely three days' worth of fish left, at the rate she had been eating. Two chunks a day, close to two pounds. Snowshoeing mile after mile, pulling the toboggan, building snow shelters, and gathering firewood— all added to her body's demand for energy. Just staying warm burned up a lot of calories. She would be wise not to wait any longer before laying in another store of fish, and she was anxious to set some rabbit snares. The fish had become hard to swallow; it never quite satisfied her hunger anymore. She would gather more cattail roots.

Willa removed her parka, spread it under the mummy bag, and zipped herself in. She felt the hard flare beneath her, unzipped and adjusted the parka, blew out the lamp, and settled herself inside the mummy bag again. She lay in the darkness thinking. Did the tips of aspen saplings have any food value? Maybe she would try cooking some and drinking the broth.

Soon she fell into a profound sleep. When she opened her

eyes in the dark, it took a moment for her to remember the igloo. It was time to rise. She felt for her flashlight inside the bag and unzipped far enough to look at her watch—7:20 a.m. The temperature was mild, as it had been in the snow cave.

Willa got into her snowsuit, scooted to the edge of the vestibule, and felt around for her boots. With an occasional blink from the flashlight, she laced them, put on her parka, and crawled to the entry hole. She pulled back the duffel bag and the bucket. Strong wind! As she thrust her head and shoulders through the hole, bitter cold burned and the wind tore at her hood. She pulled it forward, crawled another foot, and then retreated. Blizzard. Vicious wind and cold. She backed into the shelter again, blocked up the entry, and squatted in the darkness. How about that? She was stuck. She'd have to wait out the storm.

Willa crawled back to the sleeping shelf, slid her boots off, and lay down on her sleeping bag. She imagined small animals finding shelter, and dozed. She stuck head and shoulders out the entry hole again about nine o'clock. Damn—this was a kick-ass storm. She would go nowhere until it passed. Travel was impossible.

Willa lit the alcohol lamp and glanced about her little one-cell snow-block castle. The wind was ferocious! Would the shelter hold? Inside, there was only the faintest hint of the oceanic fury outside. She was grateful she had taken the time to bank the walls well. She was in no danger, as long as she stayed put. No danger, she told herself. The storm would blow over in time.

Eventually Willa's stomach insisted she eat. But could she use the stove in the shelter? Would the heat make a wet, dripping mess? Would it burn up her oxygen? She sat for a while on the folded cushion and contemplated. Sooner or later she would need to drink and eat.

Perhaps she could make a vent hole for the stove through the wall in the vestibule area. If she put it on the downwind side, the entry hole should let enough draft through to permit the wind to suck the heat out the vent hole. If it didn't work, she could just plug the vent.

Willa curled the cookie sheet into a cylinder and pushed it at an upward angle into the wall. After twisting and withdrawing it, she deposited the core of snow near the entry. Once the hole was as deep as the cylinder, she pushed her hand through to the outside, where the cold zapped her fingers. She inserted the curled sheet halfway into the vent hole and pushed her knit cap into it to plug it while she got the camp stove ready.

The stove started with little trouble. She removed the knit cap and put her breakfast pot on the roaring burner. The loose barrier at the entry allowed frigid air in as the wind outside blew over the vent hole and sucked air out. Oh, well. It was a tradeoff. The vestibule got colder, but she could cook. A little snowmelt ran down the wall under the vent.

Willa cooked two portions of fish. Might as well make the most of the stove while she had it going. The ceiling of the shelter became glazed. She shut off the stove and pushed the knit cap back into the vent tube. The bitterly cold draft from the entry stopped.

After eating her portion and setting the other cooked fish aside, Willa needed to pee. She grabbed the tarp, opened the entry hole, and crawled outside. The cold was breathtaking, the wind murderous. She stood in the trench and wrapped herself in the flapping sheet. It was hopeless. She'd have to get out of her parka and pull down her snowsuit in the whipping cold, then avoid peeing on herself and the wildly beating tarp. It was too much. She scooted back in. While the storm raged, she would use the smaller kettle as a chamber pot. Her steaming urine rang in the pan and thundered nearly to the top. She reached out and poured it into the snow beside the entry. It would sink into its own pit and freeze; no muss, no fuss.

Though the shelter would surely hold, fear gnawed at Willa's sense of security. She massaged her temples. Had it been a mistake to strike off across country? Should she have stayed with the plane? She remembered her attempt to burn the tree. A horrible realization struck her. Once all the snow had fallen from the branches, she could have built another fire under the same tree! She could have built up a huge pile of dry branches underneath, and—

No. No regrets. Seven days had passed before she gave up waiting at the crash site. The last plane flew over on the third day, when she tried to set the tree on fire. Staying longer made no sense.

Relax, Tiger, you're doing the right thing, came Bud's voice.

15

Staving Off Madness

Although Willa could sit up, kneel, or squat in the vestibule area, she could not sit up on the sleeping shelf. She had a choice of sitting on the folded stretcher cushion in the vestibule near the drafty entry hole or stretching out on her sleeping bag. Not unlike the space in the plane—only more cramped, and no windows. Definitely warmer.

Willa took out her flashlight, refilled the alcohol lamp, and lit it again. She looked at her watch: one o'clock.

She was worried about running out of stove fuel. Most of it she used just to melt snow. She averaged about two meals per tank; only five or six meals' worth of fuel remained. She'd have to cook over a wood fire at every chance from now on. At least the lamp, as faint as its blue light was, burned its alcohol slowly, and she had most of a sixteen-ounce bottle left. A couple of candles remained. As long as she was mostly lying and sitting, she would conserve her own energy; she wouldn't eat and drink as much.

Willa shifted on the stretcher cushion. In the silence, without the sounds of rustling about and tinkering with gear, she felt a deep hum, sensed the passing of heavy skirts of wind, alert to a groaning so low she could not hear it. The blue flame seemed to float by itself in space.

Willa found the little notebook and the mechanical pencil from the survival kit, but she hardly knew where to start. What day was it, anyway? It could be Sunday, or Tuesday. Sure, it was Tuesday. "Tuesday," she wrote. A good day for a list. "Pizza," she wrote underneath. "Cheesecake. Pot roast. Asparagus. Candles." Candles? She couldn't eat candles. She crossed that line out.

Suddenly the notebook and pencil dropped from her hands, and her shoulders shook with sobs. Thinking of familiar food had brought back how much she missed human contact, and she had an all-out cry, an empty-the-benches cry, a fans-flooding-the-stadium cry. Finally she was done; she dried her face and blew her nose in the red bandana.

She put on her parka, blew out the lamp, and crawled to the mouth of the shelter. Removing the bucket and duffel, she thrust her head out. The snow-filled wind struck her face like a sand-blaster. For an instant she saw six feet into the blur; then tears from the cold blinded her. She pinched her parka hood tightly around her face. After a moment she crept entirely outside the hut and crouched in the roaring entry pit. Snow was filling it.

She could see nothing but a dim torrent of whiteness, keening like a banshee. Wind sliced through her parka and slashed her cheeks and nose. Without the stocking cap over her face, inhaling air that cold was like trying to breathe ammonia. She quickly retreated into the snow-block fortress and sealed the entry as tightly as she could.

Safe inside, she removed her parka and opened her snowsuit. Little light penetrated the storm and the walls of her shelter. Kneeling, facing the rear, Willa could barely make out her hand in front of her. Her eyes played tricks on her. At one moment the igloo seemed to glow faintly silver like a hole in the lake ice. She closed her eyes, but the silver cave remained. Feeling unmoored, she groped for the alcohol lamp.

She lit the lamp and the interior of her lair appeared again. The small blue flame brought out dimly the maroon of her sleeping bag, the green duffel at the entry, and the red of the stove—or was she imagining the colors?

The silver vision had disturbed her. On all fours inside the ghost tube she'd begun to slip off somewhere, lost her balance, felt dizzy. What was that about? Feeling game, she wanted to go back and try it again. She blew out the lamp and waited on hands and knees, waited as the pale orange afterimage of the lamp flame danced about in front of her, waited as unwanted visions returned and taunted her. It did no good to close her eyes. She sighed and waited patiently, smelled the ripe odor of her body escaping from around her neck, listened to her own breathing, and gave up.

She lit the alcohol lamp again.

Unused to being confined, prevented from the prodigious expenditure of energy that had become her daily norm, Willa picked up her spoon and fork and turned her mess kit into a drum kit. She explored the springy trills the fork tines made on the bottom of the shallow saucepan and used the spoon on a kettle for bass tones. Tiring of that, she ran her fingers through her thick hair and felt the Gordian snarls. She hadn't touched her brush since the crash. She found the brush and set to the task gingerly but with relish. It was a rare self-indulgence, and she took her time. She didn't check her watch, but by the time she could run the brush through without snagging up, she guessed that an hour had passed. Her hair was greasy and dense.

Having pulled forgotten amenities from her little black duffel bag, she put balm on her lips and then rubbed some into her ragged cuticles. Her fingers had grown thick and rough. Holding her fingertips near the lamp flame, she trimmed her nails. Then she rummaged further and pulled out her empty compact. She didn't use powder, of course, but the compact mirror had lasted through years of packing. She hadn't given a thought to looking at herself since the accident.

She flipped open the case, bent over the dim flame, and stared at her dark image. She didn't see her face. She turned the mirror over and looked at the back of it for a split second. Then she looked at her reflection again, straining to see her features. She could see her teeth when she grimaced, but the light was too dim to make out much else. She flipped the case shut.

"Hey, let's party!" she said aloud. She ferreted out her two remaining candles, planted them in the packed snow floor, and lit them. Then she took a deep breath, opened the case again, and looked.

Her entire face was ruddy, chapped, mottled, streaked. Crusty white flecks circled her mouth like the rings of Saturn, and her nose wasn't pristine either. Her lips looked exactly like a pair of fuzzy leeches. She leaned over against the edge of the sleeping shelf. Her eyes filled with tears.

"Looks like I stuck my face in a sewer and then a blast furnace," she groaned. Her face was ruined; her life was ruined. She'd never get a date after this, she thought, blowing her nose into the bandana. Except maybe with Bigfoot. Of course, she wasn't getting any dates anyway, so what the hell? "Party on!" she said. She rubbed the tears into her cheeks and blew her nose again.

She seized the stove and set it up to make some water in the large kettle. When the snow had melted, she topped up her thermos and then added more snow until the kettle was half full. She dropped her bandana in and stirred it with a fork for a minute. Then she lifted it up, let it cool, and wrung it out. She gently washed her face, rubbed in some of the Lily Pond balm, lit the candles, and checked the mirror again. Much better. "All set to go dancin' at the Roundhouse," she sang out.

Washing her face had used a little extra stove fuel, but it felt so good that it was worth it. Willa refilled the alcohol lamp, lit it, and blew the precious candles out. Steam from the kettle rose into the vent hole. Why waste a kettle of hot water? Quickly she stripped off the top and bottom of her longjohns and got into her snowsuit and boot liners. She spread the tarp out on the floor of the igloo and then dropped her socks and long underwear into the kettle one piece at a time. She wrung them out carefully over the kettle and spread them upon the tarp, where they steamed. The air in the igloo was soon filled with fog. Washing her polyester longjohns would restore their insulation efficiency, but how long before they dried? She left the vent open to help clear the moisture out.

Wanting them to dry faster, Willa got out of her snowsuit, put on the icy cold long underwear, and then got back into the snowsuit and felt boot liners. Body heat would help drive off the moisture. She put the lid on the kettle of warm, gray water and left it near the entry to radiate its heat into the igloo. Leaving the vent open allowed cold air into the vestibule, although it was very dry air.

After the water had cooled, Willa dumped it outside the entry and crawled back onto the sleeping shelf. After lying for twenty minutes working the chest of the snowsuit like a bellows and lifting and lowering her legs to keep air moving and blood circulating, she crawled into the mummy bag and fell asleep.

When Willa woke, she was warmer. She yawned. She opened the snowsuit and ran her hands over her underwear. Except for the spots where she had been lying, it was nearly dry. What was happening outside? She looked out the vent hole. She saw a small, light patch of streaking snow. The blizzard through a periscope. Yep, still there.

Willa pushed her knit cap back into the vent tube. What was the temperature out there? She pulled her thermometer out and tied a few feet of fishline to it, pulled the vent tube out, and pushed the thermometer outside. Of course the mercury would start climbing back up the moment she pulled it in, but at least it would give her an idea. After a few minutes she retrieved the thermometer: 27 below.

Sitting cross-legged, Willa pulled her mouth harp out of her shirt pocket, blew up and down the scale to wake up her ears, and teased out a blues tune. Next she launched into a lively rag, "John Henry," which she'd learned from a vinyl LP Karin had inherited from her grandfather. She explored some old camp songs, "Alouette" and "Land of the Silver Birch." After those her mouth was tired and she put the harmonica back in her pocket.

Give me a piano, she thought, giggling at the idea of hauling one on her toboggan.

Oh, how she loved show tunes and spirituals! A few times a group of kids had gathered about the piano on the gym stage after school and sang as Willa played old standbys—rare events she savored, when her rep as a silent nerd was forgotten for a while. Willa had learned many of the tunes in the Thursday night choral group at Meeting. There was nothing dull about the Friends' taste in music, she had to admit.

She sang songs she knew and made up others until her throat grew sore. The concert had dissolved the walls of her hut, but now—there they were again. She stretched.

Leaning toward the flame of the lamp, Willa checked her watch. It was 4:30 in the afternoon. She checked the vent hole. No change there. Then, feeling drowsy, she got out of her snowsuit, crawled into her sleeping bag, and soon fell asleep.

She was walking, walking without moving, and suddenly before her was a sea of green rushes rolling in a warm wind. She inhaled deeply the fragrance of spruce and wildflowers. At her feet lay a wooden canoe. She stepped into it, and it bore her through the clicking reeds and turned into a wild goose. The powerful bird took flight, mounted through the clouds, and carried her homeward.

When she awoke, she pulled her snowsuit on, looked out the vent hole, and found that the winter storm still raged. Her watch showed a little after seven o'clock. When would it end? How much more could she take?

She tilted her head up, reached around behind, and grabbed her forehead with her fingers; then, as if her arm had gone berserk, she pulled herself onto her back over the edge of the sleeping ledge. "Yaaahhh!" she yelled at the ceiling of her snow capsule, then began chattering as if demented.

"You gonna stop the wind from blowing, eh?" she hollered. "Go ahead, hold up your hands, spread your fingers! So what ya gonna do? Hoist a sail! Oh no, not me. I'm no loon. I don't wanna fly to the moon! No, gonna stay right here, holed up with the woolly bears and the mice, thank you very much. Gonna lay low in the snow where the grass don't grow.

"Lemme outa here, Mr. Ezekiel! I can't take it anymore, gonna bust outa here, just get up and walk away, just see if I don't! Fine, fine, then, it's a card game with no cards. Your play. No, yours. How about the national anthem. Can't sing anymore. Horsed around too long, summer's almost gone. I'll say. Daylight in the swamp, Tiger.

"Yep, it's the finest dog breath around. Just check the *Globe*. Next? Are you waiting for a bus? Taxi!" Willa jabbed her finger into the cold ceiling, loosing a shower of ice sparks and spruce needles, and shrank back in terror of the roof caving in.

It didn't budge. Of course. The structure was far too massive to fall to a mere finger poke. As cold as it was, the thing had probably frozen into a single plump shell. She rested her forehead on the heels of her hands, smelled the faint smoke on her sleeves and the fragrance of the balm on her face, the sharp smell of her body unbathed for ten days, and listened to the nothingness and the millions of tiny springs ringing in her ears.

Willa pulled the uninsulated flight suit out of her duffel bag and quickly changed into it. She began doing pushups, then leg raises. She was surprised that she could continue to hold the leg raises far longer than her usual limit. Finally she stretched and rested, and when she began to cool off, she got back into the snowsuit. She felt much better. She put her boots and parka back on, tucked the stocking cap over her face, grabbed the tarp, and moved to the entry hole.

She crawled outside and wrapped the blue tarp around herself, then stood up with her back to the gale. The wind still whipped fiercely; she had to brace herself. The plastic tarp effectively cut the wind and allowed her to stay out a few minutes. She gazed about in the downwind arc into the cold, boiling storm. A nearly full moon would be rising. She could see only a few yards; venturing out in such a maelstrom could be fatal. Through the racing snow she could see nothing but the dark, hulking spruces upwind behind the hut. The fiendish cold began to numb her face and fingers; she retreated back into the shelter.

Willa ate some of the cold cooked fish with broth jelly clinging to it and sipped lukewarm cooking water from her thermos. The nearly congealed liquid made her gag, but she had to eat. She played her harmonica again and then sang "Blackbird," softly; she almost had to whisper it. When she got hungry again, around 9:30 p.m., she boiled the rest of the cattail roots and ate most of the remaining cooked fish. She slid into her sleeping bag and lay thinking of the time when she was a little girl and a wild thunderstorm had struck.

She had been lying in bed, wide-eyed, listening to the rain

thrash against the windows and the wind howl and the house creak and things outside knock and bang. Lightning flashed in the room. She clutched the covers under her chin, afraid of what she saw, but afraid not to look. Jean came in, found her awake, and whispered, "Isn't it great? I love storms! It's better than a movie, isn't it!"

They sat on the bed together, Willa nestled in Jean's lap. They talked about the nooks and crannies where the squirrels and birds found shelter. Jean told her that birds and squirrels had been surviving storms for millions of years, so not to worry. And then they lay down and went to sleep.

In the shelter Willa could hear scarcely anything of the fury outside, but she knew it was there, and its power frightened her. She felt like a mouse defying the titanic eagles of the north.

She knew mice and moles did burrow under the snow. You could see their tunnels when the snow melted in the spring. Once while skiing she had seen the meandering tracks of a small creature come to an end between a parenthesis of wing marks.

The wind was the hunter she feared. The spruce grove lay fifty yards upwind of the shelter. But spruces were not likely to let go of large branches in the wind; nothing would come crashing through.

She slept at last, and dreamed dreams that made her squirm off her cushion until cold spots underneath woke her. She moved back onto the cushion and slept again.

She was huddled with Lonnie Kingfisher in a dark, dome-shaped hut over a hole in the ice, calling or singing something. They had made the hut by stretching the blue tarp over a frame.

On a line three feet beneath the ice swam a small, nervous pike. Willa saw a large shadow pass beneath the hole, the size of a person, and grabbed her spear. The pike lurched frantically; then an enormous fish blocked the hole and Willa plunged her spear into its body. With all her strength she pulled back on the spear and wedged it in the hole, while the monster thrashed and thumped against the ice, gradually quieting.

Electrified, Willa shifted the spear; the thing thrashed some more and became still. Willa peered down in the hole as she kept the spear pressed to the side, and saw a sturgeon, an ancient giant with a line of welts running along the middle of each flank from gill to tail. Could she even bring it up through the hole? She turned to ask for help, but Lonnie was gone. It would be a tight fit. She got its snout partway up the hole, where the fish became stuck. Wearing her heavy mitt, she reached down into the water, grabbed the monster through the bottom of its gills, and pulled. It was very heavy; she was barely able to pull it up through the hole. She dragged it outside. It filled her toboggan; the tail hung out of the rear by a couple of feet. It looked like a prehistoric punk of the deep, with its rows of studs and the barbels on its chin. She made her way slowly off to the southwest, lugging the sturgeon. She heard muffled laughter, and when she looked back, it was Lonnie lying in the toboggan.

When Willa woke up again it was only 4:30 a.m., but she was alert. She quickly slipped into her boots, snowsuit, and parka and went to the entry hole. She removed the bucket and duffel bag, crawled warily through the opening, and stood up. Stars glittered, and the moon hung near the northwestern horizon, surrounded by a large halo. The storm had passed, but the cold was intense, and with the stiff breeze, travel would be dangerous.

She stood up, shielding her face with her mitts. Looking around, she saw scattered trees near and far, silhouetted against the snow. The stars were thronging in the black sky. Riffs of snow skated along the ground.

The searing wind drove her back into the shelter. She lit the alcohol lamp and fired up the camp stove to fix breakfast. After pondering for several minutes, she concluded that it was Day Twelve.

16

The Storm Lifts

Willa watched the snow shrink from the sides of the kettle and slowly soak into the water. This morning began her second day in the snow-block hut. She would go mad if she were pinned down another hour. Her mood swelled up like a thunderhead laden with hail as she stirred the pot of melting snow and thought of the tireless, forbidding wind. She wanted to burst through the walls of her shelter and go storming off across the landscape. She swallowed her fish breakfast in an irritable mood.

On the other hand, the interlude was good for body and soul. She had slept and dreamed a lot. Her knee tendons hardly bothered her at all now. But enough was enough! She would set up a windbreak outside and build a fire. But when she ventured outside, she saw the effort would be futile. As the sun edged above the horizon, her thermometer registered 33 below zero. The windchill was wicked.

Willa fretted for a while about her food stock. She had just enough fish to carry her through the next day. By noon the temperature had risen to 26 below, but the wind was still merciless. She played her harmonica, she sang, she exercised.

As boredom and claustrophobia threatened her sanity, she seized the opportunity to tune up her snowshoes. She retrieved them from the snow outside, let them lie on the floor to warm up, and then picked out knots and tightened the webbing. Enough daylight shone through the snow so that she could work without lamp or candles.

What did the rabbits eat, how did they get through the winter? They struggled to survive and perpetuate their species, and then died. People too strove to make a living, raise children, and then they died. But they also created life that lived outside them in many ways—their art, their work, their love. Was it that life that was sustaining her?

Of course, people fought and made war, too. She pulled a cord taut and retied the knot, working half by feel, half by sight in the low light. People ran away, they hid, they abandoned. They fell through the ice.

Wolves in the wild taught their young things they couldn't learn in captivity, like how to hunt. And beavers built complicated lodges and engineered habitats with dams. Wasn't that a kind of art, an industrial art? On a summer canoe trip with Bud and Jean they'd watched a pair of martens play like slapstick comics, jumping and tumbling with each other. Willa had nearly burst with the effort to keep from laughing out loud and scaring them away.

God, she was hungry. She took a sip of water from the thermos.

And everything that lived, died.

Look at the aspen trees. Their roots joined together into one system. An individual tree would die, but its roots remained to suckle the community. Wasn't it odd that aspens, which lost their leaves in winter, were the trees that were flexible enough in the cold for her to make snowshoe frames with their wood? Spruce should be more flexible, being so full of pitch.

Willa noticed that the seatbelt bindings were slightly worn where they looped under the cross ribs and came in contact with the snow and ice. Since the straps were plenty long, she simply slipped each one through a few inches so that new material was exposed on the bottom.

So many people had been part of her life, and she part of theirs. A braiding and unbraiding of lives. Where did one stop and the other begin? Maybe people were like aspens, with their hidden, interconnecting roots. Something underneath, something that had always been there, kept growing, kept going on, even when someone died.

That evening Willa knew that she faced serious trouble. She was eating her next-to-last meal of fish. She'd had to use up her reserve during the storm. Instead of trapping a fresh supply, as she'd planned, she'd been trapped in the shelter. Now her first priority was to find a site to put down her fish trap.

After she had eaten and refilled her thermos, she ventured outside one more time before bedding down. The temperature had climbed a few more degrees and the wind had calmed. Not very much new snow had fallen. She prayed that the weather would allow her to move tomorrow. She couldn't stand another day confined to the igloo, and she desperately needed more fish. A huge clamshell-colored moon had risen.

Again Willa woke well before dawn. She crept outside and was greatly relieved to find that the wind remained calm. The temperature was still very cold, 15 below, but the sky was clear and the sun would warm things up. Her spirits lifted by her liberation from the snow shelter, she built a roaring fire, pulled out a tongue of coals, and cooked her breakfast. While waiting for the snow to melt in her pot, she turned her sleeping bag inside out and held it up to warm it before the fire. She wanted to drive out as much moisture from the insulation as she could before packing up.

When the fish was cooked, she ate, squatting near the fire. Although the taste was no more exciting than sawdust by now, it was sustenance; the forkfuls of flesh were warm and nourishing. It was her last meal until she weaseled more from the cold wilderness. In this land of lakes and streams Willa was confident that she would soon find another site where she could trap another load of fish. She stood up. Where was the toboggan? It had the fish trap on it.

Oh, God! Where *was* the toboggan? Willa scanned her environment in the moonlight. The toboggan was gone! Dumbfounded, she walked forward ten paces and stopped. There it was, snagged under a bush. She laughed. It was all right, easily straightened. She'd tie it down from now on.

She packed up her gear and set off again in a south-southwesterly direction as the stars glittered above. In the east the sky was growing light.

At sunrise she was startled when the snow in front of her exploded and big white birds fled to the treetops. They were ptarmigans—a species of grouse that buried themselves in the snow and hid beneath the surface, breathing through a tiny hole. One of those would make a tasty dinner. But the way they hid in the snow, how would she ever catch one?

When the full light of day had returned, she entered a broad muskeg. Small, stunted spruce grew scattered about, like a kindergarten of trees. By noon, feeling tired, she stopped to eat the last morsels of fish. She had not yet seen a single place where she might set her fish trap.

But as her rhythmic steps rustled into the afternoon of her sixth day of traveling—her thirteenth day since the crash—Willa came upon a snow-covered stream leading from a small lake. At last a possible spot for the trap.

She untied her shovel and retrieved her ax from the toboggan, cut an aspen pole about eight feet long, and walked out upon the lake. First she would test the ice at the head of the stream and use the pole to see how deep the water was. As she reached the spot, she shoveled away the snow and began chopping a hole in the ice with her ax. With the first blow, the ice cracked and gave way beneath her. Willa fell backward, and saw to her horror that the ice was only an inch thick, covering a fast, olive-black current.

She heard and felt the ice cracking beneath her. Water already burned her left leg as she threw the ax ahead of her and churned herself across the snow away from the hole like a startled crayfish. She crawled several yards toward the bank, rose to her snow-shoes, and loped away. The ice was thin near the middle of the narrow channel; it thickened toward the shore. She sat in a drift and packed snow around her soaked leg to absorb as much of the water as possible, nostrils flaring and chest heaving with the pain of massive cold and fear.

Willa rose and stood for a moment, her arms held out as if she were suspended by the nape of her neck. She had to start a fire right away and dry out her clothes. She shuddered, as much from the close call as from the icy wetness. The chill gripped her like a vise. She drew the toboggan into a cluster of jack pines and began gathering wood, moving briskly, her leg already crusted with ice.

She lashed a pole across two trees near the fire site at chest level and tied her tarp up to serve as a windbreak and ground cloth by the fire. She made another dash around the area to gather all the extra firewood she could find, because once she started the fire she would have to take off her wet snowsuit, longjohns, boots, and socks and dry them. She had no extra boots. Her left foot was numb and her knee was stiff. The snowsuit leg was already as rigid as cardboard.

Willa dug a fire pit in the snow and moved deliberately to prepare the birch bark and sticks. She was shaking badly, very frightened. A couple of attempts to light the birch bark failed, but she had the cattail fluff in her pocket. Kneeling over the shallow pit, she made a nest of the fluff and with cold, clumsy hands shredded the birch bark into fine strips and held the lighter flame to it. *God almighty, take, take!* Her entire body quaked like an ancient alarm clock going off. She squeezed herself still, her breath bursting in jets of steam. The flames took. She fed them slowly and carefully. *Jesus, please burn, please burn.*

In time the fire came along and breathed on its own. She carefully added small sticks, waited, and then added larger ones. Sitting on the tarp, Willa got out of her boots and clothes; then, standing momentarily half naked, she put on her flight suit and parka. Now for her feet. She removed the liner from her dry right boot, slipped her foot into her stocking cap and put the boot back on, then put the liner on her left foot. She pulled the empty oatmeal bag out of her duffel and tied it over the liner. Now at least she could hobble around a bit. Thankfully, the temperature had climbed during the day, and the air was hardly moving. She would be miserable for the next few hours, but with a fire going she'd make it.

Willa set up a tripod of saplings near the fire and tied her wet boot and liner on one of the tripod's legs to dry. She hung up her snowsuit and her longjohns. She kept close watch on the fire and her clothes—she couldn't afford to let them burn. She needed more wood. Doubting that the plastic bag on her left foot would hold up much longer, she tied the empty nylon food sack over it too. She stretched and jigged in front of the fire until her shivering subsided and then hobbled about with her ax, taking only the thicker branches that she could quickly break free. As long as she kept moving, she stayed tolerably warm.

She returned to the fire with a bundle of wood and built up the blaze. She warmed herself for fifteen minutes, then went out again on a brisk circuit. Her polyester longjohn bottoms dried quickly; soon she was able to put them back on. She was colder than she had ever been in her life. She grabbed her mummy bag, slipped into it, zipped it all the way up, and snuggled down inside, squirming and pumping to warm up. Before long, though, she had to emerge to feed the fire. Her socks dried next, and then the outer boot, which was mostly rubber and leather. The boot liner and the snowsuit were still damp.

Cold and exhausted though she was, she was extremely lucky that the accident hadn't been worse. She could have gone completely into the water. It could have been 30 below zero and windy. She could have been fish food in the spring.

On the other hand, she still had no food.

After a couple of hours near the fire, Willa's boot liner was dry. The snowsuit was still damp, but Willa was exhausted, shivering, and worried she was getting hypothermic. She sure felt sleepy. In the failing light she laid out her sleeping bag on the stretcher cushion at the foot of the tarp, put on her snowsuit, and crawled into the bag. She hoped the rest of the moisture would evaporate without costing her too much warmth. After she had tied the stocking cap and bandana over her face, she pulled the parka over her as extra protection from the icy air. Tired beyond thought, she drifted off to sleep. She woke cold several times, grasped her legs under the knees, worked her muscles to warm herself, and fell asleep again.

17

Wolves Again

Willa woke tense, fighting for warmth. She unzipped the mummy bag and threw off the tarp. The early light revealed a cloudy, cold sky. She had to get some hot water in her. She pulled on her parka and boots and rose to her feet. "C-come on, Tiger, it's a n-new day!" she chattered, hopping stiffly up and down.

She pulled her snowshoes out of the snow and tied them on. After gathering an armload of sticks, she built a fire and put on a kettle of snow. She opened her sleeping bag, shook it out, and laid it out over a bush. While the snow in the pot took its usual time to melt, she shifted from one leg to the other and swung her arms around herself. The orange sun blazed through a narrow slit at the clouded horizon. She had no food. She had burned a tremendous store of calories yesterday. The ordeal sprang back on her and she dropped into a squat, pressing her hands against her temples. She could have died! But she was still here. Hungry.

She had to find another place to set the fish trap. And look for cattails.

The water was hot. She sipped it carefully from the pot until she was full, added more snow, and heated water for the thermos.

Her shaking stopped. She stood still and looked out at the

January landscape. She was driving south. Like the wolf, she was a taut, hungry creature who had to travel on, trusting her instincts.

Willa packed up the toboggan. She hitched herself to the tongue and paused astride her snowshoes. The shovel. It was still out there. But she didn't want to go near that deathtrap again.

She unhitched herself from the toboggan and trudged to the edge of the narrows. There it was. Her shovel. It was a shelter tool. She needed it.

Cut a new pole. The one she had yesterday lay out near the spot where she'd fallen through, just a couple of yards from the shovel.

She cut a long aspen sapling and trimmed its branches off, then crept cautiously within the pole's length of her shovel. There was nothing to hook onto, so she swept the pole in an arc that caught the shovel and pushed it toward shore. She picked it up and returned to the toboggan, much relieved.

On her way at last, she crossed rough, frozen bogs with shallow sinks and snowcapped tufts. She crossed frozen creeks. She passed over small lakes whose connecting streams were iced solid or were little more than winter-stilled marshes. By noon her stomach reverberated. Maybe the seismologists would get a bead on her, she thought. Her thermometer read near zero. Her legs, as if separate from her, moved on. Her clothes rattled loosely around her.

She stopped at a cattail bog and dug a pit in the snow with the shovel, shearing off most of the dead stalks, and chopped up the ice with her ax. She tired quickly. She picked out chunks of ice, uncovered the muddy layer below, and fetched the bread bag from her duffel so she could reach into the forbidding water and grasp the roots. Sliding the bag over her right mitt, she noticed a gaping hole. The seam had split while she was hobbling around with the bag over her boot liner. She wouldn't be able to reach down into the water.

Unless her arm was bare. She got out of her parka and the top of her snowsuit so she could pull her shirt and longjohn sleeves up above the elbow. Her arm fried with cold as she reached into the mud and groped for the roots. Grasping a limp cord, she pulled her flaming arm out. She dropped the root, quickly wiped her muddy arm in the snow, shook it off, and pulled her sleeves back down. Snowsuit top on, parka on, mitt on. Her arm fizzed hot in her sleeve.

She shuddered. That was not going to work.

Willa tried for an hour to pry roots out with a stick, and twice she succeeded in getting one end of a six- or eight-inch rhizome above the muddy slush so that she could grasp it with the plastic bag over her mitt. Two pieces after an hour of effort. She had probably burned more energy than she would get from eating the roots. She jammed them into her parka pocket, hitched herself back up to the toboggan, and headed south toward the next lake. The sled was getting heavier.

She trudged slowly for hours, taking frequent rest breaks. By day's end she had not found a place to put her fish trap down.

Within a cluster of spruce, Willa stopped for the night and built a fire, moving slowly. She put on a pot to heat water. Leaning toward the flames, she breathed the warm, smoky air. She was very tired. Her stomach felt full of hot lead. She cut up the cattail roots, boiled the pieces, and chewed them. She swallowed the slimy, faintly sweet juice from them and spat the pulp back into the pot. She would boil the last of the starch out and drink the water.

Starving sucked.

She sat quietly on the empty bucket with her eyes closed, lungs heaving slowly, trying to push back the panic and confusion. She'd just have to move carefully and keep drinking water.

She opened her eyes. Watching the fire eased her mind. Tomorrow, keep looking for a fishing site. Be careful. Carry a pole in case of ptarmigans. Maybe she could club the last one.

Willa dug a narrow, shallow trench with her shovel, then laid out her bed with the tarp folded over the bag. No energy to build a hut. She tied her bandana and stocking cap over her face, snugged the drawstring of her mummy hood tight, curled up on her side, and waited patiently, her hands between her thighs, for her body to warm up the chilly sheath.

She wanted to move the flap of the tarp so she could see the starry sky, but she didn't have the energy to open the bag again. Had she ever been so exhausted? When her people appeared, as they always did at the end of the day, she put them to bed like some gruff ptarmigan hen, shoved them down into the snow of her exhaustion, tended to her heartbeat, and floated off in a silent black current.

She was in an operating room. Everything was white. Orderlies rushed down mazes of white tunnels pushing gurneys with bodies under sheets, leaving them in the end rooms and rushing back. She noticed that her feet were gray with frostbite, and suddenly she was being carried away under a sheet. She struggled to sit up, throw the sheet aside . . .

It was morning. Willa rose up on her left elbow in her sleeping bag, and the blue tarp rattled. She unzipped the bag and pushed the sheet aside. What day was it? She couldn't remember.

Willa dressed, melted snow, sipped hot water. Every task took a million seconds. Warm again, she packed her gear, laced it down on the toboggan, and snowshoed away, already fatigued. Her hunger no longer resided in her belly but burned in every cell of her body.

She shuffled on, lugging the toboggan. She stopped to sip water from the thermos. The overcast sky pressed down. The fox spoke softly to her. *Eh, death isn't so bad. It will be like going to sleep. You'll have rest.*

A bent cattail stalk rattled like a dry throat in front of her. She stopped. Shook her head and walked on. *No, ain't ready yet, not by far.*

"Ain't gonna go, oh no, oh no, ain't gonna go toda-ay," she sang out. "Gonna push on through this snow, this snow, ain't gonna stop, no way. That sweet chariot can just swing on by today." She slogged on, using the sapling pole to steady herself, and the tin toboggan loaded with gear tugged along behind her.

She came upon a matronly spruce robed in snow. Its lowest branches arched down to the drift on the ground and formed a cove underneath. It beckoned her. She unhitched the toboggan and squatted on her snowshoes in front of the dark opening.

Her breathing slowed. So tired. Need to rest. She slumped, sitting back on her legs. Her head dropped, her eyes closed. Lights swirled, rusty sparks of fatigue.

She untied her snowshoes, stuck them upright in the snow, and crawled into the cove. With her parka hood drawn close, she curled up beside the trunk, looked out at her snowshoes thrusting from the drift, the nose of the toboggan showing behind them.

She felt like a rabbit hiding in its warren. She closed her eyes and relaxed. Was this going to be it? Had she survived to this point on so slender a thread? Had she managed so much only to die under a tree?

Why not? Life was just a throw of the dice, wasn't it? Luck, dumb luck. Now good, now bad. After all, she could have died bringing the plane down. Why not then? Or suppose she hadn't found the right spot to trap fish? And she might make it home and still die under a tree someday. Why not now? What if she lived another day, another year, another fifty? What was the difference when death was forever?

She yearned for Jean, Bud, Jordy, her friends—all the community of her beloved. *Sorry, so sorry.* She felt shame, shame that she had let them down. She lay in the dark shadow and wept. *I don't want to die. I don't want to die.*

Willa woke with her bandana frozen to her forehead and her eyelashes frozen together. She cupped her hands over her face and breathed into them until she could remove the bandana and open her eyes. Gently she rubbed warmth back into her cheeks and brows.

She had slept for over an hour. Shivering, she crawled out from under the tree, swung her arms about, and danced sluggishly in place. She needed heat inside her. She scouted about and gathered wood for a fire. The kindling took up a delicate flame and slowly persuaded the cold, hard sticks to do the same. At last her water marbled and steamed, and she drank the warmth into her mouth and throat and stomach and stopped shivering.

It was a luminous moment.

When she stood up again, the world wobbled a little, dizzy. Her mind was alert, but she felt like a bird. No thoughts, no words passed through her mind. She only looked upon the world and noted what stood there, what stirred there.

After a while Willa was ready to move on again. She willed each step as she started out. She staggered a bit now and then, steadied herself with the stick.

The world wore an aura. The edges were round; soft colors played in the snow. Her ears rang. Willa moved slowly, rhythmically along.

After a couple of hours, having made her way across a lake, Willa sat down on the big duffel bag on the toboggan and rested, breathing heavily. Her track stretched behind her in a long, broken arc. She caught her breath about the time she felt chilled, and she rose and began moving again. She wanted to stop and crawl into the sleeping bag, but she scuffed on. To rest was to grow cold.

Keep moving. She had to keep moving.

She trudged up a long slope, and the toboggan's weight pulled her back. She pushed into the cord at her waist and drew the toboggan along through deep snow, exhaustion seizing her legs. She moved them slowly forward, one step at a time, sinking, lifting, sinking, lifting.

As she reached the crest of the rise, she raised her head and was stunned. A small pack of wolves—five of them—were feeding on a carcass not thirty yards in front of her. The wolves seemed stunned as well, for a moment. Willa's adrenaline surged. The wolves burst apart, loped a few strides in the snow, then turned and snarled back at her, ugly and threatening. The raised hackles, canine teeth, and stretched lips paralyzed her. One wolf, lips pulled back, took a step toward her.

Willa felt the pole in her hand, turned suddenly, and smacked the toboggan sharply. The crack sent the wolves back a little farther, but they were reluctant to leave the meat. Her heart pounded furiously. Willa slung off her mitts, reached inside her parka, and pulled out the one remaining flare. How often she had felt it beneath her as she lay on the parka.

She barely breathed as she held the nearly invisible flame of a butane lighter to the fuse. Her heart thumped in her neck as the fuse sparked and the flare began to hurl pink fire. The wolves scattered toward the horizon, lurching and bobbing through the deep snow.

Willa retched, but her shrunken stomach had nothing to offer. She coughed and tasted sharp bitterness. Her mouth was dry, her spittle like cotton. She lifted a pinch of snow to her lips and wetted her mouth. Shaking, she stood with the flare spewing from her hand and looked at the sprawling, bloody red mess of bone, meat, and hide. An old cow moose. The wolves were out of sight. As the miracle of this gift settled upon her, Willa looked at the flare in her hand. "So who are you, eh, the Statue of Liberty?"

She planted the flare in the snow and walked over to the kill. Good meat remained; no wonder the wolves hated to give it up. Though sorely tempted, Willa knew she must not eat any of the meat raw—the old thing was probably infested with parasites.

Staggering slowly about, lightheaded, she gathered wood, dug out a pit, and built a fire. She cut away a slab of the freezing bloody meat and held it to the fire on a sharpened stick. When it had puckered brown and dripping, she held it up and gingerly chewed off a hot corner. Juices and saliva ran down her chin, and tears ran from her eyes. The meat was tough but delicious. Nothing existed then but the chewing of meat and the swallowing of juices. Nothing existed but the gift and her cosmic gratitude.

She washed down with hot water the last meat she dared take into her shrunken stomach. Her belly ached, but the pleasure suffused her bones. The vision of the snarling wolves haunted her, and she built up the fire. As the flames leaped up, Willa howled.

The rest of the meat she cut into chunks. She boiled them three or four at a time in the large kettle and then allowed them to cool on the cookie sheet. Later she'd bread them with snow, as she'd done with the fish, and stow them in the pail. Her mitts were smeared with blood. Although she dared not eat any more meat yet, the fragrant broth tempted her. After lifting the last chunks out with a spoon, she put snow in the kettle to cool the broth and sipped the rich liquid. Then with her ax she crushed the larger bones against a tree trunk and boiled the fatty marrow out. By three o'clock she had filled her pail over halfway with meat and congealed fat. The remaining broth could freeze in the kettle and she'd have it for breakfast.

Willa walked until the carcass was half an hour behind her and then chose a spot to make camp. Resting often, she dug out a drift, finishing well after sunset. She hoisted the meat bucket high in a tree and built a roaring bonfire to celebrate and to warn predators away.

The nourishment of red meat coursed through her veins as she stared into the flames. The presence of the wolves had new power, but the smell of fire would keep them at a distance. She knew it. At last crawling into her sleeping bag inside the snow-drift, she dropped into deep slumber.

18
The Winter Road

When she woke in the early darkness, Willa made a fire and thawed a ragged chunk of moose meat in hot snow water. She poured the broth into her thermos, then sliced the meat into ribbons upon the cookie sheet and reheated them with a dollop of fat. Rich aromas rose from the blackened pan. As she chewed each rope and shred of the cooked muscle of the elderly mother moose, she thought about what day it was. Maybe fifteen or sixteen. She had lost count.

The sun emerged above the torn edge of treeline and rose into a clear sky. Lasers of orange shot across the blue snow. Her soul flooded with warmth. She packed the toboggan and stood enthralled, for the first time in many, many days, by the majesty and silence about her. A snowshoe hare ventured into view.

Willa fastened her gaze upon him. "Think you're safe now, eh?" she said. The creature looked at her; then a puff of snow took his place. His trail stitched into the trees.

With the meat she had, she could see forward a week. The fat was as good as maple syrup on buttered pancakes. Willa was jazzed.

She checked the quivering sliver on her compass, even though the lakes and rivers never tacked much from south-southwest.

When she crossed a large lake she tended to veer to the left. From now on she'd needle a tree or a gap on the other side of any large expanse and home toward it.

Around noon she checked her compass again. The river she was following had taken a turn to the west. She wanted to go south, so she began navigating by the compass. The lakes were growing larger.

Near three o'clock in the afternoon, she crossed a snow-clogged land bridge and walked down a riverine neck onto the frozen plain of a lake, grateful for the firm crust. Her speed more than doubled. Forty-five minutes later, after she'd crossed two-thirds of the lake, a dark, angular shape came into view on the far shore. Probably just a rocky outcrop.

As she approached it, her heart fluttered, for the shape began to look like a building. She quickened her stride. Sure enough, it was human-built, a cabin. Another ten minutes brought her close enough to see the snow drifted against the door. She saw no smoke, no tracks, no sign of a recent visit.

In the yard of the cabin Willa unhitched herself from the toboggan and untied her shovel. It was a small, crude structure made of logs, no windows—just a hut with a corrugated tin roof. She dug the snow away from the door, removed a deer antler prong from the rusty hasp, and pulled the door open. On the dirt floor lay thin drifts of snow that had filtered through the gaps between the logs. Against the wall to the left was a bunk made of saplings, filled with dried spruce boughs. In the center of the room was a rusty sheet-metal stove with a flue pipe rising through the roof. A galvanized metal pail sat empty beside it.

A shrine it was. As simple as it was, the place was radiant. It was a monument of human design, a work of human hands, a trace of civilization. She sat down on the bunk and gazed about. The only light entered through the open door and the many crevices between the logs. She watched her breath, her mind crackling with expectation.

Two strokes of luck out of the blue—first the moose carcass, now this trapper's cabin. Of course she would spend the night. But should she hole up for a while? She could make a home here; it would be her castle in the woods. But the cabin might be many, many miles from the nearest village or road. She would spend the night and push on in the morning.

Someone's work. Human hands.

Willa went out with the metal pail, gathered wood, and filled the pail with dry sticks and strips of birch bark. She made a fire in the stove and put a kettle of snow on. When the water began to steam, she laid in a block of meat and a lump of fat. The warmth from the fire liberated a piney aroma in the cabin, and soon she could smell her sweet supper. She removed her parka, tossed it on the bunk, and sat down on her five-gallon bucket near the stove. She would like to stay in the cabin, but it didn't make sense. Of what use was a castle in the middle of nowhere? She would move on in the morning.

When the pot boiled, she let it cook for a few minutes, then set it on the floor. She speared the meat with a fork, cut off pieces with her knife, and slowly chewed the gristly fare. Last she drank the broth, which had lenses of melted marrow floating upon the surface.

If she stayed, what would she do here but wait? And wait for what? The meat and fat from the moose had restored her energy, and she could make good mileage on it. The weather was good. Better to move on than eat up the meat while fishing. The fish wasn't nearly as good a fuel for traveling anyway.

Though she lay under a tin roof, Willa slept deep in stardrift that night. In a dream the simple hut grew into a medieval fortress of log and rock, and Willa stood before a grand fireplace dressed in full armor, invincible but lonely. Turning, she walked out into the woods and waited in a moonlit clearing. A young cow moose appeared, then a she-wolf, a rabbit, a fox, a ptarmigan, a crow, all of them calm, without fear, and patiently waiting. Willa removed her armor silently, piece by piece. Last she took her helmet off and set it gently on the ground.

She awoke before light and opened the cabin door to a fine silence. A sparkling mist hung in the moonlight, like earth's frozen breath. Somewhere, not far, people slept under soft blankets.

In the gray light Willa chewed greasy moose meat and drank hot broth to which she'd added chopped spruce needles. Meat, even tough meat, was a lot easier to eat day after day than fish. It was flavorful, it was chewy, and it fed her furnace. The aromatic spruce needle oil cut the tallowy aftertaste.

She packed the toboggan, tied the tow rod to her waist, and strode away from the cabin through the woods, checking her compass. Amid the trees the early sun was hidden from view, and all was in deep shadow. At 10 below, the air snapped softly around her eyes, and her breath billowed from the bandana across her face.

Willa paced mile upon mile, stopping to sip cool broth from the thermos. Late in the morning, in the middle of a stretch of muskeg, she spotted something like a plane on the horizon ahead of her. Might have been an eagle. On she trekked through the snow, the toboggan tugging behind her. Emerging from a stand of aspen, she looked across a small lake half choked with cattails. A ridge of broken snow appeared just beyond the far shore, partly hidden by brush.

As she drew near the ridge, she grew puzzled. She came up to it, clambered over the bank, and found herself standing upon a plowed lane. Her jaw dropped. It was a winter road! It was people! They could be five miles or a hundred in one direction or the other, but they used this road!

Jordy had told her about this—that the government built roads each winter across frozen bogs, lakes, and land where none existed in warm weather. Contractors used heavy equipment and water tankers to compact and grade snow and ice. They plowed snow from wide swaths across the lakes to help the ice freeze thick. The roads connected native villages scattered across the vast, roadless reaches of northern Ontario. Willa had never visited any of the settlements, but she knew that when the roads melted, the only access was by air and canoe.

Every hair of her head pushed against the parka hood. Retrieving her navigation chart from the duffel bag, Willa squatted on the compacted snow of the winter road and spread it out. Winter roads weren't shown on it, but the larger native villages were. A northeast-southwest stretch of ice road like this one could be anywhere. She still could not locate her position on the map. Never mind!

The winter roads led like the branches of a tree out of Pickle Lake, which was a hundred miles by air from Summer Beaver, Lansdowne House, and Fort Hope, a hundred fifty miles from Webequie. She'd been on her way to Peawanuck, came down somewhere around two hundred miles from her destination, give or take fifty miles. Somewhere northeast of those settlements, Willa figured.

She had no idea whether a village lay closer to the north or to the south, but she decided to keep moving south. Maybe before the day was out, someone would drive by.

Now she had no more need for snowshoes! She took them off and tied them on the back of the toboggan. Without them her feet were so light that her muscled legs wanted to run. She walked like an overcharged bionic metronome for half an hour until she realized she was sweating and relaxed into a steady pace.

Suddenly, as if her slow-motion heart had caught up to her fevered brain, tears sprang. Willa wept as she realized that she was not hallucinating, that she really was on a road, that safety and reunion were waiting for her. Thoughts of voices and hugs made her break madly into a trot, the sheet-metal toboggan fishtailing behind her. Again she had to bend herself to a sustainable pace. Sweating was still a bad idea; she might meet no one in the next thirty or fifty miles. She strode on with a steady, rolling gait she hadn't known for weeks.

Expectancy grew—and with it impatience. The road seemed endless. She felt like an ant crawling on the undulating ribbon of compacted snow. Again she settled into a rhythm and kept a steady pace. She walked and walked and walked, and the treetops drew the day across her mind.

What day was it? She guessed it was her eighteenth day. She'd taken off and crashed on a Thursday. So it was four days past a Thursday. It was Monday. She'd be late for school. Willa giggled and felt how thirsty she was. And hungry too.

She stopped to heat up some meat. She dug into the bank of snow beside the road to make a cove where she could squat with the stove out of the breeze. Amid the noise of her shoveling she did not notice a vehicle approaching. Startled, she looked up to see a shiny, dark blue pickup with a matching topper coming to a stop and three native people peering at her through the windshield. A dog in the back began barking.

As Willa stared, forgetting to breathe, the driver, a middle-aged man with thick, iron-gray hair thrusting from his cap, got out and walked around the front of the truck. He looked at Willa, at the toboggan, and nodded at her. "Boozhoo," he said, his thick black eyebrows squeezed tightly together.

"Boozhoo," she answered. She knew that meant hello. Talking with a person who was actually standing in front of her was very strange. She couldn't think of what to say.

"You're the girl, that pilot that disappeared?" he asked. Willa looked at him.

"You survived, eh! It's the girl from Sioux Lookout that went down!" he said to his companions, who had opened their door.

"Welcome home," he said, sounding far away. He stretched his arms out to Willa and she leaned into his embrace. Her ordeal was over.

"You okay?" he asked, stepping back with his hands grasping her shoulders. His eyes were moist.

"—Yes!" Willa answered.

The other two men, not much older than she was, had edged near. "You've been in the bush a long time, eh?" said the small one. "Almost three weeks, eh? You made it out! Let's give you a hand. Here, come and get in the truck." He took her gently by the elbow and helped her into the pickup.

The men quieted the dog and stowed Willa's toboggan, with the snowshoes, shovel, and fish trap attached, in the back of the truck. One of the young men sat on the lap of the other, a fellow of great size, and Willa was squeezed in next to the driver. She had come upon the road just twelve miles south of the village of Webequie and had walked ten or twelve miles toward Lansdowne House, which was still another forty-some miles south. The driver turned the pickup around and set off as fast as the curving, rutted winter road allowed, thirty or forty miles an hour.

"I'm Gilbert Wasakezick, eh," he said, "and this is my son, Andrew, and that's Herb Kakekayash."

"Glad to meet you," said Willa. "I'm Willa Raedl." She spoke softly and thickly; her face was stiff from exposure. She was not altogether certain that this was not just another dream.

A country tune on the radio ended and a woman's voice announced, "This is CKYW Nibinamik Radio—coming up next . . ." Gilbert turned the radio off.

"Your lip's bleeding," said Andrew, who was sitting on Herb's left leg.

"Eh," said Willa, sucking her lower lip, "bloody smiling." They all laughed.

"Those snowshoes—pretty good job," said Andrew.

"Thanks."

"So, the basket—what's up with that?"

A look from Gilbert cut him off. "So—what happened?" asked Gilbert. The muscles in his brow rippled. "Engine trouble?"

Willa reached back—it seemed so long ago. "Well," she said, "the battery melted, and the storm . . . Cabin was full of fumes, half my instruments were gone . . . Radio was gone . . . Had to bring her down."

She shuddered and went silent. Her lip was bleeding again.

Gilbert put his arm around her. "Look, sweetheart, it's okay, you don't have to talk now."

The heater was blowing in her face. "Could you turn this down," she said, "I—I'm gonna be sick."

Herb reached over and turned the heater off.

"Thanks," she whispered.

The last eight miles were a straight track across a lake, and Gilbert sped up to seventy, slowing only for a couple of pressure ridges. The pickup pulled into Webequie and Gilbert slowed down by the clinic. It was closed.

"I'll take you to my house," said Gilbert. "My wife's the chief," he added. "We'll call the nurse over, eh?"

As they entered the house, Gilbert spoke rapidly to his wife in Ojicree, the regional blend of Ojibwe and Cree, and picked up the phone.

Gilbert's wife, Darlene—Dar—pulled a chair back from the table for Willa and took her hands. "Miss Raedl! Please, sit down! You have come back from the dead! They had a dozen planes and hundreds of snow machines out there looking for you. Everybody pretty much gave up hope a week ago after that big storm. Will you have a cup of tea? This is our daughter, Katie."

The house was very warm. Willa looked at the Wasakezicks' daughter, wide-eyed and shy, and smiled, making her lip bleed again.

"Yes, thank you," Willa said. It was all so dreamlike.

Gilbert called the nurse. Willa removed her parka, draped it over the chair, and unzipped her snowsuit to the waist. She sat down and loosened her boot laces.

"We heard all about you," said Dar. She poured steaming water into a mug in front of Willa and dropped a tea bag in it. Willa was in a trance.

"After Gilbert gets hold of Sally, the nurse, you can have the phone," said Dar. "Make whatever calls you want. We have a pilot, but his plane is in the shop right now. You probably want to call Sioux Lookout, eh?"

"Thank you," said Willa. "I want to call my parents, and then I should call Search-and-Rescue or something, I guess."

"That's all taken care of, dear. Let me see your hands. How are your feet? Let's take your boots off."

"I don't think that's a good idea," said Willa, wrinkling her nose. "They feel fine."

"Anything you want?" Dar continued. "Hungry? You must be starved. Katie, put that bannock on the table and get some butter out of the fridge, would you, hon?"

"Thank you," said Willa. She liked Katie. Katie looked about twelve. Willa buttered a slice of bread and took a large bite. The expertly made quickbread, a simple staple of the local diet, was such a joy to eat that it brought tears to her eyes. Gilbert set the phone in front of her. The long cord was twisted like a wild grapevine.

"Sally went to her mom's. Regis went to get her," he said to Dar.

Willa called home.

"Hello?" Bud's voice.

"Daddy!" she croaked.

"Willa!"

"Daddy, Daddy, yes! I'm at Webeq—" Her voice cracked in a sob.

"Are you all right?"

"Yes . . ." The word came out in a whisper. "I'm all right, I'm okay. I'm so happy to hear your voice."

"Willa." Bud's voice was quaking. "I can't believe it, thank God!" The line was silent a moment and Willa heard a muffled sob. "Willa?"

"Yes, Dad?"

"I just can't believe—oh, sweet Jesus, is it really you? You're at Webequie? Look, honey, I'm going to hang up so I can get a plane to you out of Pickle. Mom's not here—Mrs. Falkner isn't doing too well. Give me the number there, sweetheart . . ."

"Okay, Dad," said Willa, and she handed Gilbert the phone.

"She's in real good shape, Mr. Raedl," said Gilbert.

A steaming bowl of stew was set before her. She placed her hands on the edge of the table and closed her eyes. She inhaled the aromas, sifting them like sips of memory. She thought of the steady pace of her endless walking, across miles and miles of frozen lakes and snowfields, and then she felt herself being carried and laid on a couch, felt a quilt being tucked around her. Gentle fingers putting warm cream on her face. Murmuring voices melted into the swishing of footfalls in the snow as in her dream she continued her journey.